Catching Falling Stars

Karen McCombie

SCHOLASTIC

Scholastic Children's Books
An imprint of Scholastic Ltd
Euston House, 24 Eversholt Street, London, NW1 1DB, UK
Registered office: Westfield Road, Southam, Warwickshire, CV47 0RA
SCHOLASTIC and associated logos are trademarks and/or
registered trademarks of Scholastic Inc.

First published in the UK by Scholastic Ltd, 2015

ISBN 978 1407 13889 3

A CIP catalogue record for this book
is available from the British Library.

Printed by CPI Group (UK) Ltd, Croydon, CR0 4YY
Papers used by Scholastic Children's Books are made
from wood grown in sustainable forests.

1 3 5 7 9 10 8 6 4 2

www.scholastic.co.uk

For Bryn

SEPTEMBER
1939

Goodbye, Don't Cry

I stand shivering on the doorstep and take a deep breath.

Sticky toffee.

Milky chocolate.

Treacle-ish liquorice.

Like every kid who's grown up in this part of north London, I'm used to the sugary sweetness that lingers over the whole neighbourhood.

At the end of the day, shrieks ring out in our little terraced street whenever parents and older brothers and sisters come home from the Barratt's factory and hand over broken and misshapen treats they've sneaked in their pockets.

But that's not going to happen today, since there

are no children around to shriek and suck on shards of peppermint or striped rock.

They're all gone.

Every child in the street, every boy and girl in my class at school.

It's as if the Pied Piper came and stole them all away.

But they're not stolen – they're about to be hidden.

Clutching suitcases, gas masks and brown paper bags filled with sandwiches, they'll clamber on to waiting trains, which will chug them to unknown destinations in the countryside. By tonight they'll all be tucked up in bed in sleepy villages and towns far from London, and far from the bombs Adolf Hitler plans to send to our city any day now.

They'll be safe.

All except Glory Gilbert and her little brother, Richard, whose names *aren't* on the lists of evacuees.

That's because when it came to it, Mum and Dad just couldn't bear to part with me and Rich, especially while the sky stayed empty, and free of danger.

Well, that's the reason they gave, but of course *I* know the *real* reason we weren't allowed to go...

"Your face looks funny, Glory," says Rich, playing hopscotch with himself on the pavement and landing on every crack. "What's wrong with it?"

"Saying goodbye has made me a bit sad, that's all," I tell him, though that's not the whole truth.

The whole truth is sometimes too much for Rich, since he's only six and quite a nervy boy.

So if I told him how I was *truly* feeling, it would probably frighten and worry him. He doesn't need to know that saying my passing goodbyes to everyone just now broke my heart. Or that my chest aches with disappointment, thinking of the adventures my classmates will have without me. Or that I'm frightened and worried myself, of big things like bombs and small things like what's going to happen with school, since most of the teachers have gone away too.

"Don't be sad, Glory! *I'm* here, and I won't ever leave you."

Poor little Rich; he has no idea that *he's* the reason we've been left behind.

Because of his nervousness, because he's different enough to be bullied, my parents decided he wouldn't be able to cope with a new life filled with strangers.

3

"Thanks, Rich," I say, twisting the damp handkerchief that's in my hands.

Rich smiles happily, unbothered by the fact that we're all alone, the only children in a street full of adults – unless you count our big sister, Lil. But at sixteen she's all grown up, working shifts alongside Dad. In fact, any minute now, they'll be heading off to the factory, where they'll push up their sleeves, Dad minding the machinery, Lil filling sherbet fountains and cutting long rolls of pink seaside rock.

"Glory?" says Rich, flopping down on to his scraped, bare knees and pulling his beloved felt toy duck from the pocket of his long shorts. Duckie takes a turn hopscotching along the pavement – helped by Rich – and does a better job of it.

"Uh-huh?" I murmur in reply, wondering what question Rich has for me.

His mind has a habit of skipping from subject to subject and sometimes it's hard to keep up. It drives his teacher scatty.

"Did you want to be vacutated like your friends, Glory?"

"*Evacuated*," I correct him, avoiding his question. Not telling the whole truth is one thing, but if I say "No, I didn't", it's a downright lie.

"Of *course* your sister didn't want to go!" booms Dad, and I turn to see him striding out of the door of our flat and along the stone-flagged passageway, shrugging his jacket on. "We Gilberts stick together, don't we? Oi, Lil! Hurry up or we'll be late!"

Well, Dad might not be right, but at least it saved me from fibbing.

"I'm coming!" I hear Lil yell back.

Her yell is immediately followed by the usual *thud-thud-thud* from the flat above, as Mrs Mann – our elderly neighbour – stamps on the floor, letting us know in no uncertain terms how much our family annoys her with our noise and jabbering.

I bet she'd have *loved* it if me and Rich had been evacuated along with the rest of the local children. Still, she'd have been stuck with Lil and her habit of turning the wireless up loud when one of her favourite American swing bands comes on.

At least we know there's *one* thing that Mrs Mann hates more than us, and that's the roost full of chickens that Mr and Mrs Taylor keep, in the garden that backs on to ours. When the hens start their clucking and crawing, it's only a matter of moments till we hear a window whack open and a roar of "Can't you keep those creatures *quiet*?"

"Hey, what are we all doing out here?" Mum calls out, coming out of the flat ahead of Lil, her hands busy with her apron as she wipes flour off them. "It's chilly with the door open, you know."

"They're waiting for *me,* of course!" I hear Lil call out, and turn to see her sashaying along the passageway as if she's off to a dance instead of the factory floor. "They want to cheer and wave me off, don't you, peasants?"

Lil can't help herself; she always grabs the chance to be cheeky. But I adore her anyway. How could I not, when I have *her* to thank for my name? If she hadn't called me Glory ever since the moment she stuck her head in my cot and met me, I'd have everyone calling me *Gloria*, like the grumpy great-aunt I was named after.

"Hold on." Dad suddenly frowns at Lil. "*Tell* me you're not wearing rouge on your cheeks, young lady!"

"Of *course* not, Dad," my sister assures him. "I'm probably just a bit flushed because I've been rushing around. . ."

As Lil lies herself out of a telling-off, I'm vaguely aware of a dull droning sound, but don't take much notice till I feel a small hand slip into mine.

"Glory, Glory, Glory?" murmurs Rich, gazing up at the plane passing overhead.

He always says my name three times – like a charm – whenever he's worried, nervous or excited. And looking down into his long-lashed eyes now, I see pure *dread*.

"Dad?" I say urgently. "That's one of ours, isn't it?"

Dad glances from me to Rich to the plane in the sky.

"Yes, yes it is," he confirms quickly. "It's definitely one of ours – you can tell from the markings. See?"

"Course it is," Lil joins in. "So everything's all right, Rich!"

"But why is it up there? Why is it even flying?" Rich starts fretting in earnest, moving from one foot to another. "Are there German bombs coming *NOW*?"

"No, son," says Dad, putting a hand on Rich's shoulder in the hope of calming him. "There'd be an air-raid warning if anything was happening. The pilot is probably just on his way from one airfield to another."

"But what if it's not? What if this is the proper war starting and the air-raid siren is *broken*!" Rich frets on, his eyes filling with tears. "Or – or the man who works the siren could be off sick and—"

"Shh, Rich," says Mum, crouching down in front of him and running a hand tenderly through his hair. "Everything will be fine. We've got our nice, strong Anderson shelter in the back garden, haven't we? And as long as we're together, we'll be safe; safe as houses. No bombs from Mr Hitler will bother us, I promise!"

"Mum's right," I say to Rich, squeezing his hand gently.

But the fingers of my *other* hand are crossed, hoping that Mum can keep her promise...

ONE YEAR LATER

2

Together Apart

"Bluebells, cockleshells!" my little brother sing-songs to my skipping, as he sits on the doorstep with the sleeping black-and-white kitten in his lap.

This one is Buttons. Its sister Betsy – the tabby – is curled up asleep on the top of the Anderson shelter in the back garden.

Rich got them both last week for his seventh birthday. It was quite a birthday; the kittens arrived and our big sister left, just like that.

"I'm off to do my bit for the war effort," Lil announced to Mum and Dad, her suitcase already packed and in her hand.

"I've joined the Land Army, and they're going to train me to help our hard-working farmers tend their livestock and crops, while all the young men are off fighting for queen and country!" she cheerfully explained to Rich.

Dad raged at Lil for not discussing it with him and Mum first *and* for lying about being eighteen to the Land Army recruitment officer, when she's really only seventeen.

Poor Mum was beside herself. "But we're meant to stay together as a family!" she'd said, reminding Lil of the promise she'd made Rich on the day of the evacuation, almost a year ago.

Lil just laughed, her eyes bright and her cheeks rouged pink, and kissed Mum on the forehead.

"Ta-ta for now!" she'd called out. "I'll write soon!"

We're still waiting to hear from her...

"Just a couple more minutes, Rich, and then we'll go indoors and help Mum, all right?" I pant, breathless from jumping over my skipping rope.

There's a huge pile of washing on the kitchen table. With no Lil around, I should give Mum a hand – she's been ever so busy since she started at the parachute factory.

Till last week, Lil was employed there too. Working with the silk and the sewing of the parachutes took her fancy when Barratt's swapped from making dolly mixtures and aniseed balls to assembling gun parts as part of the war effort.

Dad stayed on, though. And nowadays he's no sooner home and had his dinner than he's off changing into his civil defence uniform so he can go out on watch for enemy aircraft.

"Yes, all right," says Rich, stroking the kitten as he starts up with the skipping song once again. "*Bluebells, cockleshells...* Aw, why did you stop, Glory?"

I've let the rope go slack in my hands because we're being stared at. Hard.

A stout old lady dressed in drab shades of brown is stomping towards me and Rich, with a laden wicker basket in the crook of one arm and a newspaper tucked under the other.

"Hello, Mrs Mann," I say politely, but I know I'm wasting my time.

Our upstairs neighbour will *always* find something to moan about. Specially when it comes to my family. Mum says we could be Mr and Mrs Archangel Gabriel and their three angelic kids, and she'd *still* hate us. "We'd be playing our harps too loud, or littering the yard with too many feathers or something," Mum joked.

"Pavements are for *walking* on, Gloria Gilbert!" Mrs Mann says sternly as she reaches us.

She knows that Glory is the name I answer to, which is why – of course – she *never* calls me that.

"There's no law that says you can't play on them," I feel like muttering back at moany Mrs Mann, but I don't, since Mum brought me up to always be polite, no matter what.

"And how you two children can be smiling at a time like this, I really don't know..." Mrs Mann moans on, holding up her newspaper, as if that should be a lesson to us.

The paper's folded but I know what the headline says; I saw it earlier when I went to the shops on an errand for Mum. It's about the bombing that's been going on at airfields around the country.

Dad's been talking to me about it too. In this whole year since war's been declared, Hitler's never bothered sending his Messerschmitts to London. People in the newspapers and on the radio; they've called it the "phoney war", 'cause there's been no fighting here, no trouble at all.

The *real* war has been happening far away, in countries safely across the sea from us – and so lots of evacuees have been drifting back home to the city.

But in the last few weeks things have changed.

German bombers have targeted ships in the English Channel and even some coastal towns – and now Hitler's decided to take a pop at the planes and runways of the Royal Air Force. That's what today's papers are full of.

Dad says we're not to worry, though; the RAF are doing a top job of seeing off the Nazi planes.

So if Dad says we're not to worry, then I'm not going to let moany Mrs Mann scare me.

"The war will be on our doorstep any day now, mark my words!" she barks as she disappears into the passageway.

"Ignore her! Silly old moo," I say to Rich, pulling a face at Mrs Mann's back. "*Bluebells, cockleshells...* Uh-oh. What's wrong?"

I stop skipping again when I see the panic in my brother's eyes.

"Glory, Glory, Glory?" he says, shuffling nervously from one foot to the other. "What was she saying? What does she mean? Are soldiers coming? Will there be shooting? Is the war here at last?"

"No, not at all," I say sharply, and grab my brother's hand. "Let's go inside and see Mum, shall we? Maybe if we ask nicely she'll give you

15

some money for that new *Wizard* comic you wanted. . ."

I've got to act fast and get my brother indoors and distracted, 'cause once Rich starts panicking, it's incredibly hard to calm him down. He'll spiral into tears and screams and then the net curtains will start twitching like billy-o, with neighbours either sympathizing with our family for having such a peculiar, nervous child, or tutting about his ridiculous behaviour.

Thankfully, at the mention of his favourite comic, Rich gives a little hiccuping gulp, and I see I've got his attention. This might be all right if—

WEEEE-oooooo-WEEEEEE-oooooo-WHEEEEE. . .

A sudden ear-bursting, heart-stopping whine blasts through the air, the sound rising and falling ominously.

Me and Rich, we're both frozen to the spot.

"It's fine," I tell him in a firm voice. "It's just an air-raid warning. It hasn't meant anything before; it probably won't come to anything *this* time either."

"GLORY! RICH!!" Mum calls urgently to us through the passageway.

"Coming!" I shout back, realizing that me and my brother have to get to the shelter and fast.

16

We run inside and for a second – after pulling the front door of the flat closed behind us – the sound of the siren is thankfully muffled. Then it whines painfully loud again as we dive through the back door and into the yard, where Mum stands in front of the arch of the Anderson shelter, beckoning us both to bend down and hurry inside the low entrance.

"Quick!" she says, a tendril of dark hair escaping from under the scarf tied around her head.

Rich, clutching Buttons, dives in first. But I pause just long enough to scoop Betsy from the top of the shelter, where she's hunkered on the thick layer of earth and growing veg that covers it.

"Betsy!" Rich calls out from the gloom of the shelter. My eyes haven't got used to the lack of light yet, but I manage to plonk myself down on the scratchy wooden bench beside him. It's not hard; the shelter isn't exactly roomy.

"Oh, no ... no, *no*!" comes Mrs Mann's voice from the far end of the wooden bench opposite. "We are *not* having dirty animals in here, thank you very much!"

What moany Mrs Mann just said; it would be funny if Rich wasn't getting upset again. The shelter has a damp earth floor, rust blooming on the corrugated metal "walls" and a soggy, musty, metallic smell like the inside of our bin. I'd rather bury my face in Betsy's or Buttons' fur *any* day than spend time in this rotten, dank hole. Specially when I've got to share it with Mrs Mann.

I don't even know what she's doing here. She doesn't usually come to the shelter; she likes to hide under her kitchen table.

"Shoo, shoo!" she shrieks, as if the kittens were rats on the loose instead of our beloved pets.

"No!" yelps Rich, trying to scramble after a scampering Betsy and Buttons.

But I've caught my brother by the back of his long grey shorts, and Mum is already fastening the wooden door shut.

"The kittens will be fine, Rich," she says quickly. "I just saw them run inside. They'll be cuddled up under the bed in a minute, all nice and safe."

No, they won't. Mum's lying – she didn't see Betsy and Buttons run inside because I pulled the back door closed behind me, even though I shouldn't have. Dad told us that if a bomb struck a building, it was better to leave the doors open so the force of the blast could escape, and less damage would be done.

But I'm not going to think about that, because no bombs have ever come near us.

I'm not going to think about the fact that Mum is now sitting on my right in the darkness, reaching for my hand and squeezing it tighter than she ever has.

"Glory, Glory, Glory..." Rich mumbles on, burrowing himself into my left side.

"It's fine, it's all fine," I say softly, soothingly, hoping he can hear me above the siren's insistent wail.

"Huh!" harrumphs Mrs Mann, from her bench. "I doubt that *very* much."

For an old lady, her hearing is amazingly good. And my eyesight's improving; with the light seeping in from the top and the bottom of the badly fitting shelter door, I can *just* make out the shape of her in the corner. She's like a walrus. A fat, grunting, bad-tempered bull walrus. Maybe that's why she's here; she's got too big to go crawling under her table.

"I'll thank you not to frighten the children, Mrs Mann," Mum says in a voice that's tight and tense.

She's probably thinking about Dad at work, hoping he can get to the public shelter quickly.

"Me? You're accusing *me* of frightening the children? Well, I've never heard the like," grumbles

Mrs Mann. "*I'm* not the one who has put my children in danger, Mrs Gilbert. I'm afraid it's *you* who has stubbornly refused to send your children to safety!"

Moany Mrs Mann is always rude in a righteous way, as if only *her* opinions matter and everyone else is being foolish – and she's only too happy to tell them so. But this is the rudest I've heard her be. Mum is going to explode, I know it.

"Shh!"

Shh? That's *all* Mum has to say?

"Don't you try and shush me, Madge Gilbert! If you can't accept friendly advice—"

"Shh!" Mum tries to quieten our ignorant neighbour more insistently. Our neighbour who's as friendly as a scorpion living in a gorse bush.

"How dare you—"

"QUIET!" Mum hisses at Mrs Mann.

"Glory, Glory, Glory," Rich whispers in a voice so tiny only I can hear it.

I go to squeeze his hand when I hear him whisper another word.

"Listen."

And now I can make out what Mum's been trying to tune into. The reason she's been shushing

Mrs Mann. Mrs Mann must hear it too – she hasn't barked back at Mum.

It's a droning sound.

It's getting louder by the second.

It's become a frenetic drum roll in my chest as well as a noise in my ears.

It's right above us, and—

WHAM!

For a split second I'm in the eye of a storm: there's a deafening crack of thunder, a burst of lightning, and I'm being thrown upside down by a twister and spat out again.

Stillness.

I'm not where I was.

There's no bench under me, just heavy, hot … *things* on top of me.

Rich and Mum aren't holding my hands any more – my fingers are buried in stones and earth.

I can't see anything but pitch darkness.

I can't take a proper breath because of the smoke and dust.

I lift my head and try to scream but I don't have a voice, only a shrill ringing in my ears.

Overwhelmed with shock and exhaustion, every breath shallower and more difficult to draw in, I let my face fall back on to the bumpy surface where I'm sprawled. I'm so weak. Maybe I should just close my eyes, drift into deeper darkness, let whatever happens happen...

But my cheek is resting on something soft. Something made of felt and stuffed with wool.

Duckie.

Duckie is with me but Rich is not.

And now I'm clawing, fighting my way through rubble and dirt. A second ago I was limp as a jellyfish washed up on shore, but now I'm a fierce lioness, tearing at whatever's around me, roaring though I can't hear myself.

Rich needs me. I'm not going to stop till I find him.

Together we'll escape – from whatever this is – and feel cool air in our lungs and warm sun on our faces.

I hope...

Here But Where?

Butterflies.

Twirling, dancing butterflies.

Dozens of them bob and weave outside the window as the bus pulls up and grinds to a halt. One lands on the glass, its white and apple-green wings opening and shutting like angels' wings. I put my finger up on my side of the window, trying to connect with it, but it flutters off to join its friends.

Isn't it a bit late in the year for butterflies?

"Thorntree! Anyone for Thorntree?" the bus driver calls out, making Rich jump beside me.

My brother's always been nervy but he's been jumping at everything lately: Betsy or Buttons trying to leap on to his lap, the jangling bell of the scrap man coming down our road, kids cackling and shouting out in the street. All of that's got him more twitchy than usual.

It's no surprise, though. It's only been a couple of weeks since we were blown up.

"Thank you, driver!" Mum replies, getting to her feet and brushing sandwich crumbs off the skirt of her smart blue town suit. "Come on, you lazy lumps!"

She's talking to me and Rich, of course. We're both tired from the long journey, on two bumpy, rattling buses, staring at the view for hours as the London suburbs gave way to Essex countryside.

Standing up from the long back seat we've been sitting on, my legs feel as weak and wobbly as a newborn kitten's.

"Glory, Glory, Glory?" says Rich, who's been huddled between me and Mum all the way. "Are you scared now too?"

Oh, he's seen me stumble.

"Not a bit!" I lie brightly, hoping he doesn't see that my hands are shaking too. "I've just got pins and needles, that's all."

I hope Rich believes me. On the way here, I told

him how excited I was, how I was looking forward to all the adventures we'd have. I didn't tell him that the reason I couldn't finish my paste sandwich was because my tummy was in such a knot with nerves that I thought I might be sick.

"Quickly, my darlings!" Mum chides us.

Rich shuffles over so that I can help Mum pull suitcases and bags from the rack above, then the three of us try to exit the bus without battering passengers as we go. (I see some of them staring at Rich. He does look quite strange, with his one black eye and the eyebrow above it mostly burnt away. They should see the *rest* of him.)

But at last we're off, with the bus door clattering and creaking shut behind us.

I put down the suitcase and awkward brown paper parcel I'm carrying, and dig about in my bag for my gloves. The weather's still Indian summer warm, but Mum told us to pack for chillier weather too, and right now I'm glad of the gloves in particular. The string of the big parcel is cutting into my fingers. Though I'm actually glad too that I have all this awkward luggage; it gives my shaking hands something to do.

"Where's the pavement?" asks Rich, staring down

at the bare, brown earth beneath his polished leather boots. He's speaking too loudly – Mum had to keep shushing him on the bus – because his hearing is pretty bad after the blast. Mine was bad too, but I'm getting back to normal. As normal as I can be after what happened.

"Thorntree is just a little country village," Mum tells him, as she lifts a hand to tidy her already tidy, rolled hair. "Things are different here, Rich."

Now that I'm kneeling, I see that my brother's long socks are slipping down. I reach over and hoist them up, so no passers-by can stare at the fiery pink patches on them. At least the clusters of blisters have healed now. They made him look like he had some strange tropical disease.

"And what's that smell?!" Rich asks, wrinkling his freckly nose, unbothered by me sorting him out (because I *always* sort him out).

Now I smell it too. It's not the sugary scent of the sweet factory; it's the lingering stench of boiled vegetables, or something very like it.

Glancing around, I see a collection of old houses, shops and buildings, all huddled around a village green, with a large, sprawling oak tree and a small, lily-pad-dotted pond. And hovering over the green are swathes more butterflies. I've suddenly remembered what they're called, and at the same time spotted where the smell is coming from.

"Cabbage whites," I murmur.

"Oh, my goodness, yes!" cries Mum, catching sight of the sea of knobbly round cabbages growing where there'd normally be grass. "Well, that's the biggest vegetable plot *I've* ever seen."

"Is it for the war effort, Glory?" Rich asks me. They talk about nothing else at school. Everything is for the war effort; there are special bins outside the playground for scraps of paper, cloth, glass and metal. There's even one for food scraps, to feed pigs.

Not that Rich will be going to back to his school for a while. . .

"Yes, it's for the war effort," I tell him as I start gathering up our luggage, like a packhorse.

It's ever so quiet round here, I think, gazing about and not seeing a single person. It's like a ghost town, with the white butterflies as flitting, tiny spectres.

"Will we be eating cabbage a lot?" Rich asks, his skinny, bruised face crumpling with concern. He hates cabbage.

"I'm sure there'll be lots of other lovely things to eat, Richard," Mum reassures him as she begins to walk, following some scribbled instructions on a piece of paper in her hand. "Right, come on; I think it's this way. . ."

Gas mask boxes bashing our hips, we trundle behind her, sneaking a peek into the grocer's shop window with its stacks of tantalizing tins. They're piled so high you can't see inside.

"'Pass The Swan, and take the lane on the right'," Mum reads from her note.

"I don't see a swan, Mum," says Rich, looking over at the pond as we follow her. "There aren't even any ducks!"

"Not *that* kind of swan, Rich. It's the name of this pub," I tell my brother, nodding at the building we're coming up to. It's a proper old-fashioned inn, peppered with small windows – just the sort of place you could imagine a highwayman staying in centuries ago. A sign sways on creaking chains above the open door, but the picture on it is so faded that you can only guess that the flakes of paint once showed a graceful swan.

My heart lurches when I spot that we're being watched. Well, that *I'm* being watched. From one of the pub's upstairs windows an unsmiling, scrawny-looking girl is staring at me, elbows on the windowsill, pale-coloured eyes roving over me.

But what's to see? I'm nothing special. A thirteen-year-old girl in a flowery summer dress with a white Peter Pan collar. Grey socks. Buckle shoes. Bobbed brown hair held back on one side with a slide.

Maybe she's staring because I'm wearing my winter coat on a warm day, since I didn't fancy carrying it.

Or maybe she's gawping at the vivid, puckered scar on my right cheekbone.

"We must be near the farm," Rich suddenly calls out gleefully. "I can hear a pig! *Oh, piggy-wiggy, where are you, oh piggy-wiggy, where are you. . ."*

As Rich breaks into a silly little sort-of-song, the staring girl gives a sudden, snorting laugh, and then disappears inside.

I feel the faintest flurry of dread. It's not the friendliest of welcomes, after all.

"Rich, it can't be the farm *quite* yet," Mum says with a smile. "According to Vera, we have to walk quite a way down the lane before we get to Mr Wills' place."

Vera works alongside Mum at the parachute factory. She came around to see us the day the after the bomb fell, and went from tut-tutting over the mess the broken glass had made in the back rooms to rolling up her sleeves and helping Dad clear the place up.

She wouldn't hear of Mum getting out of bed to make tea for her; in fact, *she* made the tea, and came to serve it to us on a tray, with a cake she'd baked and brought specially. What a sight me, Mum and Rich must've been; all huddled together in my parents' big brass bed, a bundle of clean cotton nighties and pyjamas covering messed-up and bloodied skin.

"You know what I'm going to say, don't you, Madge, love?" Vera had said kindly, reaching over to pat Mum's hand.

"I think so," Mum had replied, though it hurt her to talk, since she'd taken a blow to her jaw in the blast.

"The kiddies can't stay here..."

Not with the planes now aiming for London, ready to drop their cargo on us all, Vera meant. I think she was trying not to say the words out loud, for Rich's sake, but he was curled up asleep with Duckie, his small body – dotted with scars, blisters and burns – trying to rest and heal itself.

"I've been chatting to your Norman, and he agrees with me," Vera carried on, her voice turning matter-of-fact as soon as she noticed Mum crumble, her eyes filling with tears. "And I've sorted something out for you."

She passed Mum the paper with a name and address on it.

And here we are now, walking down the country lane to the sanctuary of a farm that belongs to some relative of Vera's husband, George. There *had* been talk about the schools around our way doing a mass evacuation again soon, but after what happened, Mum and Dad just wanted us gone, out of harm's way, as quickly as they could arrange for it.

So this morning we had the difficult job of saying goodbye to Dad before he left for the factory. "Here; buy yourselves a treat!" he'd said, and me and Rich stared down at the shiny silver sixpences he pressed into our palms. Before we knew it, he was hugging the breath out of us both and then hurrying off with a gruff "Take care," shouted over his shoulder.

"Will there be cows, Mum?" Rich asks, bumbling clumsily along with his bags and boxes.

Yes, Dad will miss us dreadfully, but he won't miss questions like this. Those questions Rich asks over and over again when he's anxious, no matter how well they're answered.

"I think so, but I'm not sure," Mum says for the hundredth time. "Vera's never visited the farm, so she doesn't know if Mr Wills grows wheat or beanstalks, or keeps sheep or elephants!"

Rich laughs, and the laughing means he'll stop worrying for a little while and won't ask his question again straight away.

"Look, there's a sign up there – what does it say, Rich?" I ask, distracting him too.

"East ... field ... Farm," Rich squints and reads slowly. "That's it! We're here!"

He runs ahead excitedly, though slowed by his clunking luggage. Mum and I smile at each other and quicken our pace to catch him up.

The sign points us down a rutted, muddy lane, with a wide gate at the end, the sort you see in fields. There are two boys sitting on it, wearing shirts and pullovers, long shorts and wellies. They watch us struggle towards them, and the dark-haired skinnier one of the two looks as though he's about to jump off and help – till the one with fairer hair puts an arm out and stops him.

Are these Mr Wills' sons? I'm confused... Vera

told us that the farmer is a widower, with one younger and one older son. But both these lads look roughly about twelve or thirteen years old, around the same age as me maybe. Does Mr Wills have *three* sons? I wouldn't be surprised. Vera seemed vague about the details. It's her husband's cousin, after all.

Beyond the unhelpful boys I can see a messy yard, littered with tractor paraphernalia, and chickens pecking at the straw and stone-speckled ground. It looks about as picturesque as the coalman's place round the corner from our flat. Or the rubble-strewn wasteland that was the Taylors' house and our back garden just a fortnight ago.

My tummy lurches in alarm. What is this place we've come to? Yes, we'll be safe from the Luftwaffe and their bombs and strafing guns, but Mr Wills and his sons . . . they're just strangers to us. How can this farm, this family, replace Mum and Dad and home?

"Hello," Mum calls out to the boys, as she daintily picks her way down the lane in her patent, high-heeled, Sunday-best shoes. "Is Mr Wills here?"

"In the field," says the fair-haired boy, lazily thrusting his thumb in the direction of a gate in the hedge to the left of us. His hair is the same colour as the dirty straw littering the farmyard.

"Right," murmurs Mum, turning to look in the field and seeing a man on a noisy tractor. "Here goes. Mr Wills! MR WILLS!!"

Nothing. The tractor chugs on.

"Glory, Glory, Glory?" says Rich, squeezing my hand.

"Don't worry," I tell my nervy, worried little brother. "He'll hear."

"He'll hear *this*."

Then my dainty, ladylike, pretty mum startles us by putting two fingers in her mouth and letting out the loudest, most piercing whistle I've ever heard.

It works! The farmer looks round, sees he has visitors and switches off the grumbling engine of his tractor.

"Where did you learn to do that?" I ask Mum, as the farmer ambles towards us.

"It's loud in the factory. Sometimes it's the only way to get someone's attention," Mum replies with a pleased grin, which changes to a look of concern when she sees that Rich has his hands slapped over his ears. "Oh, sorry, sweetheart ... I didn't mean to startle you."

As Mum bends to comfort and reassure Rich, I

find myself shyly waving at the approaching farmer. He gives his cap a tug in reply.

I feel another hot wave of alarm.

The fact is, I'm smiling. The farmer is not.

He's trudging, as if he has the weight of the world on his shoulders – which doesn't seem very friendly to me.

"Uh, hello," says the farmer as he reaches us. "Can I help you?"

He scratches at his long bushy sideburns, frowning, looking confused, as if he wasn't expecting us at all.

"Mr Wills?" Mum asks warily, as if she's wondering the same thing.

"Yes," says the farmer.

Also coming across the field towards us is a young man, or maybe an older boy – I can't tell yet.

"I'm Vera's friend, Mrs Gilbert."

The farmer seems taken aback and says nothing at first, so Mum babbles on.

"And these are my children, Glory and Richard. It's very kind of you to take them in."

Surely Mum must be getting worried by now. She must have been hoping for everything Vera promised: cheery smiles and waves, a jolly farmer, a loving father, a willing carer for us.

Not this frowning man, looking shifty, making my insides turn to jelly.

"Didn't you get the message?" Mr Wills finally says.

"Message?" Mum says sharply.

"Glory, Glory, Glory?" says Rich, leaving Mum's side for mine. "What's happening? Isn't that the man? Isn't this the right farm? Is he cross? Is Mum cross? Aren't we going to stay here? Is—"

"Shh." I try to quiet Rich's rising panic, while mine is doing the same. I pull him away to the side, so Mum and Mr Wills can sort out whatever the problem is.

"Look, I wrote to George and Vera last week," says Mr Wills, shuffling from one welly to the other. "Told them about my roof. See?"

Our heads turn to look where he's pointing, which is towards the farmhouse, its top storey visible above the hedgerows. At first glance it looks boringly normal, and then I see that one of its chimneys is missing. And I expect the chimney is now mostly somewhere inside the house, since there's a sheet of tarpaulin on the roof, not very well held down by planks of wood.

"Cracking storm came by," Mr Wills carries on. "Took the chimney clean off, and it came right through the roof, then tore down the ceilings on that side of the house."

"Well, I'm very sorry about that. But it doesn't seem that Vera or her husband received your letter, or she would've mentioned something," Mum says curtly. "But the postal service has been rather unreliable where we are. Because of us being *bombed*, you see."

Mum's bright eyes are staring daggers at Mr Wills, as if she's daring him to say what's on his mind.

"Ah, yes ... of course," says Mr Wills, scratching his sideburns again and looking shamefaced. "But the trouble is—"

"We haven't the money to fix the roof," interrupts the older boy, who's been walking across the field towards us. He definitely is an older boy (maybe sixteen or seventeen?) now I see him up close. "We've got buckets everywhere for when it rains. We can't take your kids – there's nowhere for them to sleep. Sorry."

"What?" says Mum, livid now. Her face is flushing with anger, and the bruising on her jaw is becoming visible, even though she's tried to cover it up with make-up. "Don't you *know* what my children have been through?"

She jabs a finger towards me and Rich, at our obvious bumps, burns and scars. The older boy regards us with something that might be curiosity mixed with pity. I don't like it. The farmer can't seem to bring himself to look at us at all.

Just as well, or he might see the tears welling in my eyes as it all floods back: the day, the moment, the bomb. Of course, me, Mum and Rich survived the blast with our cuts and bruises and blisters. Betsy and Buttons – who hid in the coal cellar – didn't break as much as a claw.

But Mrs Mann wasn't so lucky.

The bomb turned the Taylors' empty house into a pile of smoking bricks and flapping shreds of wallpaper. It made their chickens disappear in a puff of smoke, like a magician's doves.

It lifted up the brick wall between our two gardens as though it was light as cardboard, and threw it on the back end of our shelter, right at the spot where Mrs Mann was sitting.

Oh, how I wish Mrs Mann hadn't died, I think to myself as I blink back the threatening tears. Partly because I don't want *anyone* I know to die, even if they are mean and cold-hearted and rude like she was. But mostly it's because it's Mrs Mann's fault we're here. I know that's not really fair to her – and it's more about the bomb dropping in our garden – but it feels as if Mrs Mann's death has led us to this unknown place, where we're unwelcome and unwanted...

"My cousin's wife explained your, er, situation," says Mr Wills, addressing his words to the muddy ground rather than Mum. "And I'm very sorry for what's happened to you and your children, Mrs Gilbert. But I *did* try to let Vera know that it's just not possible to—"

"Couldn't you have tried a little harder to get your message through? Like phoning George or Vera at their work?" Mum snaps, her voice wobbly with emotion. "I mean, we've come all this way, and I'm not taking them back to London now. So what are we meant to do?"

"I suppose I *could* take the young lad," says Mr Wills, glancing up nervously at Mum from under the peak of his cap. "He could bunk in with these two..."

He nods his head at something behind us, and we turn to see the two boys from the gate, who are now standing there, grinning. Same height, same cheeky smile, with both light hair and dark worn floppy on top and shorn hard at the sides.

"Glory, Glory, Glory?" mutters Rich, but a little too loudly.

Both the boys start sniggering, and don't have the decency to stop when I glower at them.

"Mr Wills, my daughter saved her brother's life; she dug him out of the wreckage of our shelter with her bare hands," Mum says, trying to keep her voice steady.

I look away from the stupid, sniggering boys and stare down at my torn nails, which are slowly growing back.

"So I'm hardly going to have them parted now," she continues. "Good day to you."

Mum turns on her heels, which is difficult to do in the mud.

Both boys are forced to take a step back to get out of the way as me and Rich hurriedly follow her.

"Listen, I'm really *very* sorry," the farmer calls after us as we gather our cases and bundles.

"Well, that's as maybe," says Mum, her voice properly wobbling now. "But it won't keep my children from harm, will it?"

"Hold on, hold on," says the older lad, suddenly scrambling over the fence in his muddy work boots. "I think I know who you could try. Miss Saunders in the village has a big enough place."

The farmer shrugs at the name the older lad has mentioned, but says nothing. The two boys behind us just snigger some more. I throw them another sharp look, hoping to shame them in their rudeness, but all that happens is the fair-haired one whispers something to the dark-haired, scrawnier one, and they both burst out laughing. Are they laughing at my horrible scar?

Without thinking, I slap my hand over my cheek.

"Here, give me those," says the older lad, gathering up my suitcase and Mum's and stomping off down the lane towards the village. "I'll show you where she lives."

I might be lighter, carrying only the large, awkward parcel Lil insisted I take, but I'm no less clumsy as I walk, and nearly go flying on a slick of mud.

"Glory!" Rich says in alarm, as I right myself.

"It's fine," I tell him quickly, while cackles burst out behind us.

With my face on fire, I realize I've only seen three

children of my age since I arrived in Thorntree, and all of them have been as friendly as hornets.

You know, this Miss Saunders could live in a grand stately home, with horses to ride on and the finest Belgian chocolate for breakfast, but I'd still want to get the next bus home...

4

Safe – and Stranded

"No. It's not possible, Harry. I'm sorry."

I only see a sliver of the woman behind the door of the rose-covered cottage.

I can tell she's tall, and see a glint of round wire spectacles, but that's it.

The door is open so little and the farmer's son is so broad and muscly that I don't have much of a view.

"But it's your civic duty, Miss Saunders," Harry says staunchly.

We've already found out Harry's name on the way here. His brother, Lawrence, is one of the sniggering boys we met, but I'm not sure which one; I didn't look closely enough to be able to spot the family resemblance. I don't know who the other boy is. Harry was too busy asking us all about London and the bombing that was going on. He sounded ever so excited by it, as if it was the plot of an adventure film at the cinema and not our real, frightening, new way of life.

But he doesn't understand what it's really like.

Scrabbling from under piles of hot rubble, not knowing if your family is dead or alive, finding out someone has died just a few feet away from you; that's awful, shocking, terrifying, not exciting. (Poor, poor moany Mrs Mann. . .)

"I do my part, Harry Wills, thank you very much," says this Miss Saunders, obviously enjoying the conversation about as much as I enjoyed having a melting-hot nugget of shrapnel removed from my cheek soon after me and Rich stumbled out of the ruins of the Anderson shelter.

"What, because you grow some vegetables? Donate to salvage sales?" Harry practically sneers. "Well, suit yourself, Miss Saunders. I'll show these kids back to the bus stop. They should be back in London in time for bed – and the next air raids."

Harry turns and goes to pick up our suitcases, but Mum stops him.

"Thank you so much, Harry, you've been very kind, but we'll be fine. You get on back to the farm," she tells him in a calm voice. But what's she really thinking?

Harry pauses, throws a despairing glance at the face in the cottage doorway, and mumbles his byes to us.

"I'm sorry I can't be of any help to you," Miss Saunders says quietly, and begins to close the door.

That's when Mum makes a move, her delicate hand landing palm-wide by the polished brass door knocker.

"Before we go back to London, could I ask a favour, Miss Saunders?" she asks in her most lovely, polite voice. "Could the children perhaps have a glass of water and use the lavatory?"

This Miss Saunders looks momentarily flummoxed, then backs away. I brace myself for the door to slam shut, but instead it's pulled open – and we're ushered inside.

"Of course. Certainly. Come in," says Miss Saunders, sounding courteous but cool. "Won't you sit down?"

There's no hall; the cottage isn't big enough. We find ourselves walking directly into a snug sitting room, with everything neat and tidy and pretty.

At first glance, it's much like our front room at home, with a settee and armchair facing the fireplace, a fringed standard lamp and some small side tables. A wireless sits on one, similar to the set we have on our sideboard. On Miss Saunders' sideboard, however, there's a gramophone. A gramophone! Lil would *love* that.

I glance around some more and see that on the far wall, there's a small, wooden-panelled door that's ajar – behind it I can make out some narrow, steep wooden stairs.

And to the right is a passage, which leads to the kitchen, I suppose.

"Thank you so much," says Mum. "Come, Glory! Wipe your feet, Richard!"

She's using her best voice, just like people use their best room for visiting guests. Immediately Rich and me straighten up, smarten up and follow Mum's lead. This Miss Saunders might not want us, but we want Mum to be proud of us all the same.

"Er, will you have a cup of tea, Mrs. . ." the older woman fumbles.

She's as tall as Dad and has streaks of grey in her hair, like he does. It's not styled like Mum's; just a bit wiry and wavy and cut off at chin length. She tries to tuck it behind her ears as she talks, but it just springs out again.

"Mrs Gilbert," Mum jumps in. "And this is Glory, my younger daughter."

"Er … 'Glory'?" says Miss Saunders in confusion, as if Mum has just announced that my name is Boadicea or Buttons or something just as outlandish and unsuitable for a thirteen-year-old schoolgirl.

"Short for Gloria. It's a pet name that even her teachers call her. Silly, I know, but it's all she'll answer to!" Mum says with an easy laugh, glossing over my stubbornness. "Her older sister, Lillian, is in the Land Army, you know."

Mum says that last bit with great pride, which is funny, since she's never forgiven Lil for flouncing off and joining up.

Miss Saunders' eyebrows now rise with surprise above her small, wire-rimmed spectacles. She's obviously impressed. And obviously, that's what Mum was aiming for.

"And this little lamb is Richard," Mum carries on, putting an arm around my brother's shoulders. "He's gentle as a lamb too."

She's trying to let this Miss Saunders know

that Rich isn't a typical roaring, rough-playing, boisterous boy, isn't she? But why is she bothering?

"Pleased to meet you," Miss Saunders says politely enough to us, but there's no smile on her face. "I . . . I'll just fill the kettle."

Our reluctant hostess smooths the floral-patterned pinny that covers her cream blouse and tweed skirt, and walks away – clip-clopping in her sensible brown lace-up shoes – towards the passage. She looks too tall for the low ceiling, and I swear she nearly has to dip her head to get through the doorway.

As soon as she's out of earshot, I shoot a question at Mum.

"What are you thinking?" I whisper.

"I'm thinking it's worth a cup of tea and a chat," she replies, her eyes scanning the pleasant room. "Look – I noticed *that* when Harry was talking to Miss Saunders."

Mum's nodding towards the wall with the wood-panelled door to the stairs, and I notice what hadn't caught my eye at first: a framed teacher's certificate which has pride of place above a polished piano. I know that the certificate will impress Mum, and the well-looked-after piano will please her too. Mum used to play on her grandma's piano when she was a girl, and has always wished we could afford one. She'll also be charmed by the posy of roses in the small vase placed on top of the piano.

So ... Miss Saunders is convinced she's having nothing to do with us beyond a cup of tea, but Mum clearly has other ideas.

Realizing that, a knot tightens in my tummy. I don't care if that teaching certificate means Miss Saunders is probably a responsible adult, or that the cared-for piano means she's musical, or the hand-picked posy means she likes nature. She's a stranger. Even *more* of a stranger than Vera's useless, distant relative by marriage. What is Mum getting us into?

"Mum, we can't—"

A cough interrupts me, and I turn to see Miss Saunders looming in the shadowy passageway like a wary grey owl.

"Mrs Gilbert," she says, "I was wondering if the children could run across to the shop and fetch me some sugar? I seem to have run out."

"Of course," Mum says brightly. "They're very helpful."

She nudges me and Rich to stand, and Miss Saunders nods at us, as if to say thank you.

What thin lips she has, I find myself thinking. It's as if someone was in a rush to draw her mouth, and thought a flick of the wrist and a simple straight line would do.

"Oh," Miss Saunders adds, as something occurs to her, "just tell Mr Brett at the shop to put it on my bill."

Now it's my turn to nod. I reach for my brother's hand and lead him back out of the cottage.

With the door clunked shut behind us, I stop for a second, take a deep breath and get my bearings. We're standing in a tiny front garden, filled with overgrown foliage and end-of-season roses. A last bee of the summer buzzes close by. Across the narrow road is the cabbage-filled village green, and beyond that is the grocer's shop, its frontage partly hidden from our view by the branches of the oak tree overhanging the pond.

"Come on," I say to Rich, hoping he doesn't hear the unsure wobble in my voice as I lead him out of the gate and on to the road.

"Do you think that lady will give us a biscuit, Glory? I think she might be the sort of person who has biscuits. Or cake. Don't you think so?" Rich babbles loudly as we walk.

"I don't know," I say, while trying not to let the knot in my tummy make me feel sick.

"I think she might be a nice lady," Rich babbles on, skipping jerkily by my side. "She seems nice. And tidy. But we aren't going to stay there, are we, Glory?"

"I don't think so," I say, as we pass the old pub.

Now I'm outside in the fresh air, I feel hopeful that Mum will come to her senses. With us out of the way, she'll see things more clearly and realize that she can't seriously get on the bus back to London and leave us stranded here with a thin-lipped, owlish woman we don't know.

Though now I think about it, isn't that *exactly* what happened to every other evacuee. . .?

One of the girls in my class who came back after the Phoney War, she told me they had to wait in a draughty town hall while people strolled by and chose who they wanted, as if the children were all stray dogs waiting for new owners.

"Oh, that's good if we're not staying, isn't it?" says Rich, letting go of my hand and starting to chase a flitting butterfly. "I mean, I like it here, though. I like the butterflies. The pond is nice too. Having all the cabbages growing on the green is funny, isn't it?"

"It is a bit," I answer him, watching as he bounces

and skips around. I haven't seen him do that much lately. "Do you want to stay out here while I get the sugar, Rich?"

"Uh-huh," he mutters distractedly.

And then I plunge from the sunlit green into the more dimly lit shop, the bell on the door jangling noisily.

"Hello!" says a man behind a thick wooden counter. His hair is Brylcreemed and black, shiny as shellac. "What can I do for you, dear?"

My eyes adjust and I see that the shelves here are just as packed with tins and packages as the front window.

"Could I have some sugar, please?" I ask.

"Yes, of course, dear," says the man, picking up a paper bag in readiness to fill. "How much?"

I'm suddenly confused, uncertain what I'm doing. I didn't ask, and Miss Saunders didn't tell me. We were probably both a little out of sorts.

"I don't know," I reply, feeling my cheeks burn pink. "It's for Miss Saunders at the cottage on the other side of the green. . ."

"Ha! Fancy Miss Saunders having visitors."

As soon as the words are out of his mouth, it's the shopkeeper's turn to have pink cheeks.

"Not that I mean anything by that, dear. It's just that Miss Saunders is usually one to keep herself to herself. . ."

He quickly scoops sugar from a big wooden box and presents the filled bag to me, twisted shut.

"That's how much she normally takes. I'll put it on her bill."

"Thank you," I say, taking the bag and hurrying out of the shop.

Seems as if Miss Saunders is a bit of an odd fish. Mum will have found that out by now, I'm sure, while we've been away. We might be going home after all!

At that thought, my spirits lift a little, and I untwist the bag, thinking I'll let Rich lick his finger and dip it into the bag as a treat. . .

"Ha ha ha! Go on – higher!" I hear a girl's voice call out.

Glancing quickly around, I see Rich leaping, like a wonky jack-in-the-box, trying to touch or grab at one of the many butterflies in the air above and around him.

I also see the skinny girl from earlier, the one who was sneering out of the upstairs window of the pub. Her hair is dirty-dishwater brown and looks like it could do with a brush. And her bottle-green jumper and kilt-style skirt are a bit shabby and ill-fitting, as if they might be hand-me-downs worn by several girls along the way.

"Jump! No, not like *that*. Higher, *higher*!"

She's laughing at Rich, egging him on.

"I *am* jumping high," Rich yelps as he leaps. "Hey, c'mere, Mr Butterfly!"

"C'mere, Mr Butterfly!" the girl repeats.

I can't bear it. I can't bear people mimicking my brother, and I can't *stand* this place.

"Come on, Rich," I say, grabbing his hand without looking at the girl.

"Hey, what's the matter with you?" I hear her call out, but don't respond.

"Bye, bye!" Rich turns and yells to the girl, as he skips and hops to keep up with me. "Why are you cross, Glory? I was having fun!"

He doesn't understand. He doesn't always see that people are making a fool of him, which is why he needs me.

"I'm not cross," I fib, as we approach the cottage. "I'm just thinking that we have to get back."

"Yes!" says Rich, brightening. "The lady might have biscuits!"

I hadn't meant get back to the cottage. I meant home, London.

That's where we need to be, bombs or no bombs.

But then I spot something through the cottage window.

Miss Saunders is sitting stone still, owl that she is, while Mum is smiling and has her hands clasped in front of her chest.

I don't need to read her lips to realize she's saying a heartfelt thank-you to Miss Saunders.

And I don't need to be a mind reader to know that a decision has been made while we were away.

It's one that I really don't think I'm going to like...

5

What a Welcome...

"Bye! Bye, Mum!" Rich yells, waving as the bus pulls away. "Bye! Bye!"

Mum's hand is pressed on the window and she's frantically blowing kisses at us. She's all smiles, but crying too.

I'm not smiling, or crying, because I'm in shock; shocked at Mum for leaving us here. I know that was the plan. I know that's why we came here. But everything feels upside down and awfully wrong.

"Well, then," Miss Saunders says briskly, as the bus chugs off past the church.

She doesn't say any more than that or appear to be about to do anything.

I think Miss Saunders might be in as much

shock as I am. And Rich is bouncing up and down, waving too fast, like a mechanical toy that's been overwound.

"Rich, shh, steady," I murmur, resting my hands on his shoulders to help calm him down. To anyone watching, he might look happy and excited, but I know he's acting this way because he's anxious and agitated.

The last thing Mum had said to me was "I love you", but the second-last thing was "Take extra-good care of your brother, Glory". And that's what I have to do, starting now. I mustn't let Miss Saunders see how odd Rich can be, or she might go straight back to the vicar we all met with earlier and tell him she's changed her mind. That he should get out all his documents about local evacuees and their host families and take her name off his register.

Or maybe I should *encourage* Rich and his oddness, so that Mum or Dad will *have* to come back and collect us. . .

Oh, how wonderful would that be?

"Can we go home to the cottage, please?" Rich turns and asks Miss Saunders. "Now?"

Miss Saunders looks bemused, as if she's wondering what on earth she's agreed to. She pushes her spectacles further up her nose, although they're up as far as they can go. I know what she's doing; a fidget can give you a moment of thinking time. And faced with two unexpected house guests, Miss Saunders, I suppose, definitely needs a moment to gather her thoughts.

Especially when one of them has just described her cottage as "home", as if he's settled in already.

"Er, yes, of course," says Miss Saunders, and begins to stride off.

Rich does his funny little skip-hop to keep up with her, while I follow behind.

"*Oh, butterfly, butterfly, high in the sky, high in the sky! Oh, butterfly, butterfly...*"

I stiffen, suddenly uncomfortable.

"*...high in the sky, high in the sky!*"

Teachers don't have much patience with Rich when he does his sing-songing. Last year's teacher, Miss Arnold, gave him a smack on the back of his legs with a ruler for "not calming down when I asked you to".

"*Oh, butterfly, butterfly, high in the sky, high in the sky!*"

Miss Saunders is a teacher. What will *she* be like with my brother? Impatient, weary, same as the others?

"Oh, butterfly, butterfly. . ."

"Rich, Rich!" I hiss at him, trying to get his attention before Miss Saunders becomes irritated. I know I wanted to go home just now, but we can't let Mum and Dad down. I'd never want them to be ashamed of either of us.

". . .high in the sky, high in the sky!" he carries on regardless, throwing his arms in the air this time.

With cheeks aflame, I glance at Miss Saunders and see her give Rich a sideways frown; the sort that everyone does when they're thinking he's . . . unusual.

"Oh, butterfly, butterfly—"

"It's rather silly to make up a song about a garden pest, Richard," Miss Saunders interrupts him sharply.

"Butterflies aren't pests, they're beautiful!" Rich laughs, watching the cabbage whites dip and dance over the green.

"Not when they're destroying the vegetable crop that the villagers have grown for the war effort," she tells him sniffily. "At least it's nearly the end of the season. They won't be around much longer."

"Oh! Where will they go?" Rich asks her, as if he expects her to say the Isle of Wight or India or somewhere.

"They will die, naturally. And meanwhile new chrysalises will grow and the life cycle will start again."

Miss Saunders sounds exactly like the teacher she is. Rich blinks up at her, taking this information in.

"Miss Saunders?" he says, still skip-hopping beside her.

"Yes, Richard?"

"Can we go and see our bedroom *the minute* we get home? Can we?"

Miss Saunders is taken aback, unprepared for this switch of topic. She'd better get used to it; that's Rich all over.

"Well, yes. Your room," says Miss Saunders, a little flustered. "You children mustn't expect too much. I haven't had a chance to sort it out, since my mother only very recently..."

Her voice cracks a little.

"Died." Rich says the cold, hard word in too loud and bright a voice. "Like Mrs Mann."

"Rich!" I hiss.

"It's all right, Gloria," Miss Saunders says, glancing at me over her shoulder with her cold, grey owl eyes. "He's only using the correct word. I just happen to prefer the term 'passed away'."

"*Glory*," I mumble under my breath. Mum told her I only answer to that.

"Moany Mrs Mann passed away of a bomb blowing a wall down on top of her," Rich babbles on. "What did your mother pass away of?"

I feel another sudden shudder of embarrassment, same as Dad feels when Rich talks or acts just that little bit differently from everyone else. And then I'm immediately angry with myself. Me and Mum understand Rich, no one else. And with Mum gone, I'm the only one here who can stand up for Rich, translate for him, even.

"Rich doesn't mean to be rude," I begin, hurriedly catching up with them both and putting a cautioning hand on Rich's shoulder.

"Yes, well. It's very sad about your neighbour, Richard," Miss Saunders cuts in tersely before I can say any more. "Your mother explained what happened. It must have been very frightening for you all."

"Very frightening," Rich repeats, wriggling free of my hand and skip-running slightly ahead of us.

Miss Saunders suddenly does something I almost hate her for; her nostrils flare.

It's such a tiny movement, but I've see it often

enough to understand what it means. Already, she's confused by my brother to the point of dislike. I bet she doesn't approve of the sing-songing and skip-hopping, when a "normal" child would be sobbing at his beloved mother leaving, clinging on sadly to his big sister's side.

But I know Rich is covering up his feelings, not sure how to let them out without scaring himself. He did it back home, after the blast, when he was well enough to leave the flat. Schoolteachers and neighbours would ask if he was all right and he would just start whistling some song he liked on the wireless, or worse still, laugh and do these crazy aeroplane impressions, arms wide, running around, making the "whee!" noise of a bomb dropping. If Dad was there he'd hang his head, not knowing where to look. If it happened in class, Mum would be told by Rich's baffled teacher.

"My mother was very lucky, Richard," says Miss Saunders, taking up his question again in her faintly sergeant-major, matter-of-fact voice. "She had been very, very ill for many years, and in the end she died quietly and peacefully in her sleep."

"In our bedroom?" Rich asks, glancing up at Miss Saunders.

"Er, yes ... you will be in her room. That's the only place I can put you."

Miss Saunders' poorly mother had been the reason the vicar — who was also the evacuation officer for Thorntree and surrounding area — hadn't been able to place children at the cottage when everyone left London this time last year. I'd heard that much when I was in the vicarage sitting room, while Mum and Reverend Ashton and Miss Saunders had discussed me and Rich as if we were a couple of parcels to be signed for and handed over.

"So your mother die— *passed away* in *our* bed?" Rich carries on questioning her.

Oh, no. Now he's realized that, Rich will *never* go to sleep in there! He'll have a tantrum and Miss Saunders will see the worst of him and—

"Well, yes," Miss Saunders says crisply.

"Quietly ... peacefully..." Rich repeats the words Miss Saunders used about her mother's death. "That's nice. It sounds like a nice room."

I think I know my brother, and then he goes and surprises me. How can he like the idea of cuddling under the blankets in a bed where a dead lady lay? It gives me the creeps.

"Actually, Mother's room *is* nice, Richard," Miss Saunders replies. "It has a lovely view of the garden. The apple tree is right outside and the blossom is very beautiful in May."

"I'll like seeing that!" Richard smiles up at her.

I don't know who's more surprised and unnerved by what Rich has just said: me or Miss Saunders. Blossom time is another eight months away. Surely we won't be here by then?

"Ooh, look! There's that girl; hello! Hello!" Rich calls out, spotting the cheeky girl from the pub, dangling from a branch of the oak tree by her arms. In reply to my brother, she just grins and then sticks out her tongue.

"Who is she?" I find myself asking. I must be pulling a face, because I feel a tug on the tight skin of my scar.

"I don't know her name," Miss Saunders says, sounding uninterested. She's quickening her pace now we're in sight of the cottage door.

At least Miss Saunders and I have something in common: neither of us thinks much of the girl from The Swan.

"She's just some evacuee," Miss Saunders adds dismissively.

And just like that we *don't* have anything in common.

This tall, straight-backed, unsmiling woman is simply doing her civic duty, like Harry Wills the farmer's son said she should. And she's only doing it because my mum charmed her, and very possibly begged her to take us in.

The truth is, me and Rich, we're about as welcome in Miss Saunders' spare room as an invasion of cockroaches. . .

6

No Way Home

Tick ... *tock* ... tick ... *tock* ... tick ... *tock* ...

The sound of the clock on the mantle is as loud as pebbles on a tin roof.

Rich doesn't notice. He was so bone-tired that I took him up here after tea and he was practically snoring before I buttoned him into his stripy flannel pyjamas.

But I've been curled here by his side for at least two hours or more, with dark, unhappy thoughts swirling in my head which have made sleep about as far away as home right now.

Wide awake, I finally give up and get up.

I don't want to wake Rich, so I inch out of the big bed, trying not to set the springs squeaking.

Once I'm out from under the heavy covers, the chill hits me, and I feel around in the dark for the armchair and the cardie I left on there when we got changed into our nightclothes.

Shrugging it on, I tiptoe over the wool rug and the cold wooden floor to the far wall. Feeling around, my hands land on what I was searching for: a small, cane-seated chair beside the dressing table. I lift it and place it by the window, then pull aside one of the thick chintz curtains, securing it with its matching tie-back.

And then I sit.

Sit and stare out into the black of the countryside night.

Of course, there's a blackout here, same as in London, with not a peep of a lamp or light allowed to show, in case it brings enemy planes screeching out of the sky with bombs as their unwelcome gift.

But I'm surprised by how much I can see in the moonlight. There's the long, fruit-tree-filled garden, with the big square that's the henhouse and distant rectangles in the ground where Miss Saunders' carrots and potatoes grow in the damp earth. Then there's the uneven dense outline of a low stone wall, and beyond that, fields roll endlessly into the distance like different shades of bottle-green and inky black velvet.

Even the bedroom looks better in the dark. I hadn't liked it when we saw it in the daytime, overstuffed with ornaments and doilies, banks of powders and potions, and too many mirrors to catch sight of my stupid scar in. It was like a museum to old Mrs Saunders, who'd lived and died in here. But seen in shadows, the clutter vanishes and the room seems blank. Just a box with a bed for me and Rich to share.

I feel my shoulders sink for the first time in hours, letting the strain of the day fade and my muscles melt.

"What are you looking for, Glory?" Rich's little voice pipes up from the bed.

So I woke him after all.

"I'm not looking for anything," I tell him in a soft voice, so Miss Saunders won't hear us from her room across the tiny landing. (I heard the creak and clunk of her door as she went in there not so long ago.)

What I've just said, it's a bit of a lie.

I've been lying awake looking for something all right. Looking for a way out of here. But I couldn't find one. Like I say, if we deliberately misbehave, we'd shame Mum and Dad, and I'd never, ever do that to them. And if I write to my parents and beg them to let us come back, every second we were in London Mum would be living on her nerves, searching the skies for planes, blaming herself for not being able to keep us safe.

So we're stuck with no way home ... unless Mr Hitler decides to stop this stupid war and stop destroying people's lives.

"Did you like our dinner?" asks Rich, throwing the covers back and padding over to join me. "I thought it was the best dinner ever!"

I'm used to Rich's odd ways, but even *I'm* struggling to understand what he's thinking and feeling. Since we got back to the cottage after waving Mum off he's acted like it was Christmas, his face wreathed in smiles. At home he eats like a bird, but as soon as Miss Saunders laid the table tonight, he ate everything in sight and asked for seconds.

"Yes, dinner was nice," I say, patting my lap for him to sit.

Dinner wasn't nice. Well, the food was, but the silence wasn't.

Another clock tick-tocked; cutlery clattered discreetly on plates.

Miss Saunders said things like, "More potatoes? More blackcurrant crumble?"

We said things like, "Yes, please!" (Rich) and "No, thank you" (me).

Apart from that there was no conversation. Which was the opposite of home, especially when Lil's there. She talks nearly as much as Mum, so Dad is always jokily rolling his eyes and telling us his ears are ringing.

"Do you think we'll get eggs for breakfast *every* day?" Rich asks as he settles himself down, curling his arm around my neck.

"Maybe," I answer, gently cuddling his skinny, warm body close to me. I have to be gentle – his patchwork of cuts and bruises is still tender in places. And Rich can sometimes be a bit funny about cuddles. He's like a cat; he has to be in the mood.

"I love the chickens. . ." he sighs happily.

"But Miss Saunders says you're not allowed to touch them, remember?"

Before our dinner, Miss Saunders gave us a short but stern list of house rules. Besides the one about not touching the chickens, apparently we must. . .

1) not wear muddy shoes in the house
2) tidy up after ourselves
3) help out with chores around the house
4) remember our pleases and thank-yous.

How does she think we live back in London? Like messy, ungrateful little thugs, giving cheek to our parents?

"I don't mind. I will just *talk* to the chickens. That will be nice," says Rich, resting his tousled head on my collarbone.

"You're being very brave," I tell him. "It'll be hard, missing Mum and Dad and Betsy and Buttons. . ."

I don't want to upset Rich, but I need to sense how he's doing, how he's coping inside with this strange day of ours – without letting him know that I'm struggling too.

"Oh, I don't feel brave, Glory. I just feel happy," he says matter-of-factly.

My brother's reaction is puzzling me more than ever. Being away from home, parted from Mum especially, I had expected something different. Maybe jangled nerves and overexcited babbling at best, tears and panic at worst. I just hadn't expected plain "happy".

"What's that light over there, Glory?" Rich suddenly asks, before I can work out a way to weasel into his mind some more. "Is it the dawn already?"

Sure enough, there's a soft, orange glow on the horizon.

But it's nowhere near dawn; I don't know the time exactly but there's still two or three hours till midnight, I'm sure.

And then, with a stab to the heart, I understand two things very clearly.

Rich might not know why he's happy, but suddenly *I* do. Away from the constant war chatter and sandbags and air raids of home, he's relaxing. Instead of looking out at the rubble of our back garden and beyond, today he's been laughing at the sight of knobbly cabbages on a village green, dancing with butterflies, chatting with chickens, eating two bowlfuls of hand-picked and home-made blackcurrant crumble.

For the first time in a very long time, Rich feels safe.

Which is why I can't tell him the *second* thing that I know for certain.

That the burning glow we can faintly see is London far, far away – and on fire.

"Yes, it's the dawn, so we better get back to sleep for a little while longer," I lie, standing him up and pointing him in the direction of the bed.

Before I join him, I draw the curtain and hide away the glimpse of the distant city, bombed and burning...

Glory's Gift

I'm cold, I'm wet, and someone, somewhere is sobbing.

The floor of the Anderson shelter is soaked with rain, and I don't know why I'm lying on it. Mum will know, but I need to find Rich first.

"Rich. . . Rich?"

I sense him trembling close to me, and my eyes flip open.

It's dark, but a vertical chink of light tells me I'm not in the Anderson shelter back home – I'm in Miss Saunders' mother's bedroom. I'm not asleep and dreaming any more, I'm wide awake and lying on damp sheets.

"Rich?" I say, sitting up quickly, throwing the

74

covers back to see how bad the damage is. "It's fine. It's all right. I'll sort this. . ."

Rich is curled up tight, his arms around his knees, head buried into them as he cries and shakes.

"Let me get some daylight in here," I mutter, bouncing out of the bed in a squawk of springs and hurrying to the window.

Outside, the world is green and sparkling with dew. Birds are singing. Chickens are pecking and preening. The sky is blue and cloudless – with only a haze of grey smoke on the horizon.

The sight of the smoke makes me stop dead and my tummy heaves.

How bad *were* the raids last night? And where exactly were they? Please, *please* let it be nowhere near Mum and Dad . . . not again.

How can I find out? I know; I could ask Miss Saunders to put on her wireless later, when the news comes on. Yes, that's what I'll do. Though the bomb that killed Mrs Mann never made the headlines. . .

"Glory, Glory, Glory?" whimpers Rich.

All right. Until I can find out any news about home, I just have to push the thoughts of bombing to the back of my head and try to will away the sick feeling in my stomach.

Because right now there's nothing I can do about London, and a lot I can do to help my little brother.

On the way back over to him, I catch a fleeting glimpse of myself in the dressing table: bobbed brown hair messy with sleep; pale, tired face; red spider of a scar sitting on my cheekbone. I look like I could audition for the part of a ghost in a production by the sweet factory amateur dramatic society back home.

I grab my cardigan and, with a quick fling, throw it over the mirror.

"Sit up, sweetheart," I say, as I perch on a dry patch of bed and stick my fingers under Rich's chin. Head forced up, his tear-soaked, red-rimmed eyes look pleadingly at me.

"I didn't mean to have an accident," he snuffles, wiping his nose on his pyjama sleeve. "I was just scared to go out to the privy in the dark. There are cockroaches and things in there."

To be honest, I had tried not to gasp when Miss Saunders showed us the cottage privy yesterday. At home, our toilet is just beside the back door, and is nothing special – just a white, porcelain loo with a polished wooden seat. But it's like a throne in a palace compared to Miss Saunders' privy. Hers is just a small shed in the garden, with a wooden plank to sit on. There's a hole cut in the plank, and a deep hole dug in the ground below it. If that wasn't awful enough, the door has a wide gap at the bottom, which all sorts of slithery and scuttly things make full use of. There should be a tiny welcome mat there for them.

"It's my fault," I tell him. "I should have taken you out to the loo when we were both up. Or I should've asked if we could have a chamber pot."

At the words "chamber pot", Rich gets the giggles, which is an improvement.

"Let's get you out of these," I say, helping him off the bed and pulling at his pyjama top and soaking bottoms.

I need to get him washed, of course, but before I sort that out, I need to get him warm. Glancing around the room, I see a faded pink candlewick dressing gown hanging on a peg at the back of the door. Old Mrs Saunders doesn't need this any more, but one shivering small boy does.

Rich giggles some more as he holds out his arms and the overlong sleeves flip-flap.

"Move!" I laugh, budging him out of the way as I strip the bed, and toss the sheets and blankets into wet and dry piles by the door.

Next, I haul the window open wide, then wrestle the heavy mattress off the bed and manoeuvre it over to the window. If I get a bowl of soapy water and scrub it, hopefully sunlight and a fresh breeze should help it dry out.

"Ooh, look! Look at me!" I turn and see Rich at the dressing table. He's taken a round cardboard box down from a shelf and is now wearing the contents. It's a black felt hat, a bit like the shape of a plate. A bunch of fabric pansies are sewn on one side, and a crinkled panel of black netting hangs over Rich's blue eyes.

"Rich! Take it off!" I laugh. But Rich is turning this way and that, grinning as he pings the hat's black elastic thread under his chin to keep it in place.

It's good to see him cheerful again, so I decide to let him be. Now that I've got this mattress propped up safely, I'll go downstairs with the washing and explain to Miss—

Oh.

What's that sticking out from under the bed frame? Of course; it's Lil's brown-paper parcel, her leaving present. Mum popped it under the bed when she took our things up here yesterday, while we were sitting at the kitchen table finishing our milk and biscuits.

"You must write and tell me what your silly sister's surprise is!" she'd said as we walked her to the bus stop. "Trust her to make a mystery of it all."

The mystery had started when Lil wrote me and Rich a letter, after Mum told her we were being evacuated.

Typically, it was short and sweet – Lil probably had a million other things to do, like find a way to wriggle out of working, or try a new hairstyle.

Dear Glory and Rich,
     So you're off to the countryside, just like me! You HAD to copy your big sister, didn't you?
     Have a whole lot of fun, try not to miss home too much and see you back there sometime soon.
     Rich – be good for Glory.
     Glory – don't go chasing too many handsome country boys!
     Kisses and hugs galore,
     Your ever-loving sis,
     Lil xx

PS Glory — I have a gift for you. There's a parcel at the back of our wardrobe. Take it with you. DO NOT OPEN IT TILL YOU ARE SETTLED AND ALONE IN YOUR NEW HOME! Hope you love it.

Well, I'm not totally alone — it's very hard to be anywhere without Rich by my side — so I'm just going to open it now.

"The flowers wobble when I shake my head like *this*," Rich is saying, but I'm too busy picking at the tight twine knot of the string around the parcel to take much notice.

"Hmm? Actually, Rich — did I see a vanity set on the dressing table? Could you pass me down some nail scissors if there is?"

"Here," says Rich, handing me a tiny pair of scissors with mother-of-pearl handles.

Snip.

"Thank you," I say distractedly, setting the scissors down on the floor and tearing the package open.

Oh. . .

It's as if it's suddenly growing in size.

Set free from the string and strong brown paper,

the soft, sheeny material inside puffs, flops and slithers around, like white silk lava.

"What is it?" asks Rich, sitting down cross-legged beside me.

"It's . . . it's pieces of parachute silk," I tell him, holding one ragged offcut in my hand.

"Lil gave you bits of parachute as a present?" Rich frowns, and I frown too. I know exactly what this is and what Lil's done. Mum said that some of the younger girls working at the factory would steal leftover bits of fabric and use them to make blouses or even underwear. Lil had been one of those girls, it seems. And she didn't want Mum to find out, which is why she told me to wait till I was alone to open it.

But why did she think I'd want her stolen parachute scraps? Because Lil was thinking of *herself*, as usual. She gave me a present *she* would want. Same as she warned me not to chase handsome country boys – and no guessing which of the two of us would be more guilty of that. . .

"Glory, Glory, *Glory!*"

Uh-oh. Like an air-raid warning, Rich's cry escalates from mild panic to high-pitched panic in the space of three words.

"What?" I say, glancing up sharply.

"I forgot!" he wails, tears pouring down his face. "I forgot Duckie!"

"What on EARTH...!" Miss Saunders bellows from the doorway.

I see it through her eyes straight away.

An open window, waving curtains.

An upended mattress.

Jumbled sheets and blankets in messy piles.

A slithery pool of silk rags all over the floor.

A crying boy wearing her mother's prized hat and dressing gown.

The last time Miss Saunders saw her mother's room it was neat and tidy, prim and proper.

Now it must look like a German pilot took a wrong turn after dropping his load on London and was hell-bent on destroying all traces of Mrs Saunders Senior with his last remaining bomb.

"I can explain," I say hurriedly as I stand – and instantly feel the nail scissors pierce the skin between my toes.

Howling, I crumple to the ground, only dimly aware of the red bloom on the ripple of white satin nearest my feet...

Unwanted Guests

I stare at the knobs on the wireless, wishing I dared turn it on and find out if there's any news from London.

"How's the foot?" asks Miss Saunders, as she clatters down the narrow stairs with the bundle of wet bedding in her arms. Quickly, I snatch my fingers away from the polished walnut of the wireless casing.

"Fine. Better," I tell her, though it's still nipping a bit. I'm glad she didn't see me touching her stuff. After what's just gone on upstairs, I don't dare put a finger on anything.

"That's called a *wireless*."

Oh, so she *did* see me. And she thinks I don't

know immediately what it is, as if my family is too poor to have one. Some of my old school friends who came back after the Phoney War said that a lot of people in the countryside have this idea that evacuees all live with penniless families in slums back in London.

"Yes, I know. Our one at home is a bit bigger," I say, exaggerating just a little because I'm cross that Miss Saunders jumped to conclusions and cross that she caught me out.

"Really," Miss Saunders says curtly and takes a few steps towards the passage.

"I just wondered. . ." I hear myself say, my heart pounding.

Miss Saunders stops and stares intently at me through her round wire spectacles.

"Yes, Gloria?"

I *must* ask her not to call me that. But it'll have to wait; I need to ask her a favour and don't need to make her any more riled than she already is.

"I – I couldn't sleep last night, and I looked out of the window and saw fire in the distance, in London, I think," I say fast as I can, trying to get to my request. "I just wondered if we might listen to the news? To see what's been happening?"

"I'm afraid we haven't had the radio on in this house for years. My mother couldn't bear any noise whatsoever," Miss Saunders replies. "It probably doesn't work any more."

That explains the silence of our Saturday night, I suppose. No cosy evening around the fire, listening to *The Children's Hour*, like we do at home. I bet the gramophone hasn't been touched in years either, or the beautifully polished piano.

"Anyway, I'm quite sure everything is all right, Gloria," Miss Saunders adds. "If there was any problem. . ."

Her voice tapers off. I bet she was going to say that if there was any problem, we'd have heard, that someone would come and tell us. But if another bomb fell on our street, and Mum and Dad . . . well, how would anyone know where me and my brother were? The details of Miss Saunders' address, of Thorntree, would all have been turned to dust. Neighbours might tell the authorities that they heard we were in Essex somewhere, and checks would be made, but it would take for ever for anyone to track us down and break the bad news, wouldn't it?

No.

Stop.

I don't want to drive myself crazy by thinking about all that, so instead I decide to see how Rich is getting on. Awkwardly, I push myself up off the armchair, but Miss Saunders sees and waves me down again.

"No, no. I don't want you walking that mess all over my rug, thank you very much!"

She's had enough of mess this morning, what with the upside-down bedroom caused by my brother's "accident". "A big boy of seven being scared of going to the W.C. in the dark? What nonsense," she'd tutted disapprovingly when I explained what had happened.

But this particular "mess" Miss Saunders is talking about is a paste she made of Epsom salts and hot water and dabbed on my cut foot.

I do as I'm told, flopping back down into the padded chair, my nightgown puffing as I do, and put my foot back up on the stool that's covered with an old tea towel.

"But Rich needs me," I say, pointing in the direction of the kitchen.

"I think your brother can manage very well on his own," Miss Saunders replies, giving me a stern schoolteacher-knows-best look over the top of her spectacles.

Sure enough, I can hear him singing in the tin bathtub by the range, sounding as happy in his few inches of hot water as Cleopatra would've been lounging chin-deep in asses' milk. Still, Miss Saunders doesn't know Rich like I do and he'll need me to help him get out and dried off.

"Yes, but, I think I'd better just—"

Miss Saunders sighs impatiently, realizing I won't take no for an answer.

She deposits the laundry on to the stone passage floor, then walks briskly over to me.

"Here, let me wipe that off," she grumbles, lifting my foot and the towel, and settling herself on the stool.

I feel uneasy with this arrangement, but Miss Saunders rubs away at my foot in her lap with the speed and efficiency of a nurse. Which she was, in a way, if she cared for her poorly mother for so long.

Not knowing what to say or where to look, so I find myself glancing around the room, my eyes alighting on the certificate above the piano. She catches me at it again.

"I was a teacher once," she says, gazing over her shoulder and then back at me. "But I had to give up a long time ago, once my mother became ill."

Should I say something? But all I can think of are questions that might sound cheeky, like how she can manage without working. Maybe Miss Saunders' father died too and she's been left money? I can't be that rude. Still, Mum would say it's *also* rude to stay silent when you're being spoken to.

"Did – did you teach here, in Thorntree?" I finally ask, as Miss Saunders pulls a small bandage out of the pocket of her pinny, quickly wrapping and fastening it around my foot.

"At the primary school, yes. A Mr Harris took over after me for a few years. Since he retired it's been young Miss Montague. You'll see her today; she plays the organ at church..."

Miss Saunders' thin lips go ever thinner, even more of a tight line, and I can see she doesn't think very much of the school's current teacher or her musical skills.

"Right, you're done," she announces suddenly, setting my bandaged foot down on the ground. "Oh, look at the time! With all this palaver, we're going to be late for church if we don't get a move on. Can you go and get yourself dressed and decent, please, Gloria?"

"But Rich—"

"Upstairs, please," Miss Saunders says again in her best stern schoolteacher voice. "I'll see to your brother. There's a towel warming for him by the range."

She holds a hand out to help me up, then points me in the direction of the stairs.

As I hobble over, I pause to watch as she bends and scoops up the washing in the passage. But in the second she straightens up, a look crosses her face that I don't much care for.

She's staring into the kitchen, presumably at my brother in the tin bath.

The look on her face; it's one of disgust.

My brother and his odd ways; this boy who wet the bed in her beloved mother's room, he disgusts her.

Oh, yes of course; I mustn't forget that me and Rich, we're completely unwanted guests.

To Miss Saunders, we're only a couple of scruffy, dirty evacuees who've been dumped on her...

Run Away, Run Away

"Have you settled in, children?" the vicar asks kindly.

Reverend Ashton ruffles Rich's hair as he talks.

Rich says nothing, just shyly shuffles into my side, blinking his black eye.

"Yes, thank you," I fib in a voice not much louder than a whisper.

Little does the vicar know that all I want to do is take my little brother's hand and run away, run away.

"Super! Well, why don't you have an explore while I chat to Miss Saunders?" Reverend Ashton suggests, pointing to the graveyard surrounding the old church.

I glance around and see gravestones leaning this way and that, like rotten teeth. Gnarly trees overhang them and ivy twirls up them, as if the foliage is working together to hide the dead villagers from the living ones that are streaming out of the Sunday-morning service.

The graveyard gives me the collywobbles to be honest, but I'd rather lose myself in the greenery and the ghosts than spend a minute longer being stared at by the entire congregation. At one point during the service I felt like rushing out of the pew and up into pulpit, just so I could shout, "Yes, we're strangers here! Yes, we look ugly and bruised and scarred because we were BOMBED. All right?!"

But instead I kept my head down, staring but not seeing the words in the hymn book, while Rich sang loudly and only slightly out of tune as Miss Montague, the primary school teacher, pumped out the hymn "All Creatures Great And Small" on the organ.

"Here, Gloria, Richard," says Miss Saunders, standing ramrod straight in her grey wool coat and rifling around in the handbag that's hanging on the crook of her arm. She pulls out two neatly folded brown paper bags. "Instead of loitering around here, you can make yourselves useful and gather some damsons for me on the common."

"The common?" I say. I don't know anything about Thorntree, apart from the village green that all the buildings huddle around. And I didn't know we were here to be Miss Saunders' servants and "make ourselves useful"...

"It's behind the church," says Miss Saunders. "Climb over the stile in the wall and you're there. And if you follow the path across the common it will bring you to the lane at the side of the cottage. I'll meet you back there shortly."

Miss Saunders might look like a great, grey owl, but now she's sounding like the witch from "Hansel and Gretel".

"Thank you," I say, still thinking of Mum and minding my manners as I take the bags from her. "Come on, Rich..."

I grab my brother's hand and manouevre as quickly as my tender foot allows me through the gawping throng milling around the church.

"Look, Glory – there's my friend!" says Rich, pointing. "And she's with *them*!"

His friend? "Them"? What is Rich talking about?

I glance at the faceless crowd, and my tummy does a flip as I suddenly recognize three people: the two sniggering, awful boys from Mr Wills' farm and the scrawny, cheeky girl from the pub. They stare and whisper behind their hands, as if me and Rich are animals in the zoo. I saw them in church too, turning to inspect us, their eyes boring uncomfortably into me and my brother.

"She's not your friend, Rich, and just ignore those boys," I tell him, pulling him away sharply.

As soon as we round the corner of the church I relax. We have the place to ourselves. And beyond more secretive, ivy-covered gravestones I can see the wall and the stile and the bright, pretty, tree-dotted common.

I just hope I can work out what damsons are; I've never seen one.

"Aargh!" roars Rich, letting go of my hand and bounding off into the undergrowth. "I'm a tiger in the jungle!"

"Wait, Mr Tiger," I call after him, limping my more careful way through the tangle of leaves and crunching branches underfoot. "I need to talk to you!"

But my big-cat brother has spotted the stile and scampered over it already.

"Rich!" I call out, hurrying as fast as I can, but my school shoe is a little tight because of the bandage and it's making my foot quite sore.

As I cautiously step over the stile I worry that Rich has bounded off out of my sight – but as soon as I'm on the other side I spot him hunkered down, staring intently at something in the grass.

"Look, Glory! Mushrooms!" he says, grinning at me over his shoulder. "We could gather them for Miss Saunders!"

"Stop! Don't touch anything – they might be poisonous," I warn him, hopping over at high speed.

Once I'm by his side, I peer at his find, a cluster of red-capped mushrooms dotted with white.

"They look like the ones Alice ate in her adventures in Wonderland, don't they?" Rich says enthusiastically.

"Yes, and that didn't go well for her, did it?" I say, trying to let him down gently.

And while we're here, I need to let him down gently about something *else*.

I don't want to say this after realizing how settled and relieved Rich felt last night. But I can't have him thinking everything is all right, because I don't think it is.

Not after this morning, when I spotted the expression on Miss Saunders' face as she looked at him.

"Yes, Glory, but they're very pretty and I think Miss Saunders might like—"

"Listen, Rich, I need to say something important," I begin.

Here goes.

Except I'm not sure how to put it.

How do I explain that I'm positive that Miss Saunders is telling Reverend Ashton right now that she's made a mistake; that we have to be sent back? (What *else* can they be talking about? Why would she be so keen to get us out of earshot?)

Rich blinks up at me like a sweet, sad puppy. This isn't going to be easy.

"The thing is, Rich. . ."

"*Whoooo*. . ."

We both freeze at the sound. An eerie sound like wind whipping through treetops. Only there isn't the faintest hint of a breeze today.

"Glory, Glory, Glory?" Rich whispers.

"It's nothing," I tell him, though I'm not sure if that's true.

"*Whooo*. . ."

All right, so it's *something*.

And it's coming from over the wall, from the graveyard.

"Is it a ghost?" asks Rich, clearly terrified.

"Shh, don't be silly. It's probably just—"

"*Whooo-OOOOOOO-ooo...*"

"Is it Mrs Mann, Glory? It's Mrs Mann, isn't it!"

"No, Rich, of course it's n—"

"*Whoo-aaaaaAAAHHHHH!*"

With the quickest glance at each other, me and Rich read each other's minds and know exactly what to do.

Run away, run away.

"Hurry, Glory!" yelps Rich, as he scrambles off along the path between the trees. Plum-type fruit hangs from the branches above him, but I'm not exactly in the mood to work out if they're damsons or not.

Instead I'm doing my best, ignoring my painful toe, hobbling at fast as I can after him.

And then I hear a different noise.

Definitely *not* the sort a ghost makes.

I slow down and hop-hop-hop to a stop. Up ahead, Rich turns and does the same.

"Oh, VERY funny!" I shout out angrily to whoever's giggling and laughing behind the wall. "You got what you wanted, so you can stop laughing now!"

But the people tricking us don't stop laughing.

They carry on, and then scramble to their feet and laugh some more.

And of course it's the boys from Mr Wills' farm and that girl from The Swan. Who else would it be?

"Let's go," I say to my brother, pushing him ahead of me along the path through the common, walking with my head held high and with as much dignity as I can manage.

"Do they want to play, do you think, Gloria?" Rich asks, turning to look back at the lone girl and her horrid boy pals.

"No, they just want to make fun of us," I tell him, desperate to put as much distance as I can between those mocking people and me and my brother.

Even once we're out of earshot, it's as if I can still hear the sniggering.

I hear it all the way along the path through the common, following us down the lane at the side of Miss Saunders' cottage and even up the garden path.

Tappitty-tap, tap.

This might be the last time I use this brass door knocker – it's of a fox's head, I notice. I don't suppose there's a bus leaving today, being Sunday, but if Mum or Dad can get some time off work tomorrow I reckon they'll come for us then. Reverend Ashton will have a phone – he's probably calling our local vicar or some evacuation officer back in our part of London right now, trying to get a message to our parents...

And how will poor Rich take it? Mind you, after the stupid prank the Wills' lads and the scrawny girl just pulled on us, he might not want to stay here anyway. My poor, nervy little brother...

The front door opens – and Miss Saunders, still wearing her Sunday best coat and hat, frowns at us.

"What are you doing?" she asks.

"I'm s-sorry?" I stammer.

What; had she expected us to leave already, without any of our things?

"For goodness' sake, you don't have to knock if you live here," she says, unbuttoning her coat. "From now on just come around to the back door and let yourself in."

Oh.

So we ... we actually live here? I think to myself in surprise. *We're not being sent away?*

"No damsons?" Miss Saunders asks as we come in, close the door and follow her towards the kitchen.

I think of the paper bags we must've accidentally dropped when we ran and feel guilty.

"Uh, no. We didn't see any," I tell her.

"We heard a noise so we ran!" Rich explains. "It was like a *wh*—"

"It was nothing. We just heard some children playing a game," I say quickly, stopping Rich before he tries to make the noise and starts sounding crazy.

I don't want Miss Saunders to have an even worse impression of him than she already does.

Miss Saunders frowns at the two of us as she hangs her coat and hat up on a peg by the back door. She motions us to hang our jackets there too.

"Now then," she says briskly. "I had a chat with Reverend Ashton, and he said . . . well, a few things. But most importantly, he suggests you need to start school straight away, tomorrow, so you can settle into the community. Biscuit?"

Rich dives straight into the tin she's holding out. I shake my head, still shocked to find out we're staying. What happened? This morning she was looking at Rich with disgust written all over her face, and now she's giving him biscuits, telling us to use the back door as if we're family. Did Reverend Ashton persuade her to give us a second chance?

"I have to say, Richard," Miss Saunders carries on, as she puts the biscuit tin down and starts rummaging around in a tall cupboard by the back door. "I *still* think it's silly that a grown-up boy of seven is scared to go to the lavatory in the night, and scared of gentle creatures such as spiders. But I really can't tolerate a situation like this morning again. So here; if it helps, you can have this."

She takes an old-fashioned silver torch from a shelf and hands it to Rich. His mouth goes in an "o" shape.

"It belonged to my father," says Miss Saunders. "You may borrow it while you're here, to light your way to the lavatory in the dark. But no wasting the battery, now!"

"I won't, I promise," Rich says, turning the torch around in his hands and examining it in wonder, as if he's been given a bar of pure gold.

"And here's something else. Perhaps you could take these up to your room, Gloria?" Miss Saunders takes out two items and hands them to me. The one on the bottom is a heavy rubber sheet, cold and clammy to the touch. The one on the top is a very pretty, ornately decorated potty that looks like it might be Victorian.

She's given me these to help combat any middle-of-the-night accidental wees, which is kind of embarrassing ... yet I'm strangely touched. It *must* mean she accepts that Rich is a shy little boy who might have trouble settling in. And it means she's happy – or at least resigned – to having us here.

Of course, if we're staying, I'll *have* to work up the courage to talk to her about what I like to be called.

And don't they say there's no time like the present?

"Thank you," I tell Miss Saunders; then, before I lose my nerve, I add something. "By the way, my name is just Glory. If you could call me that, I'd appreciate it."

There. Pleasantly put, and polite with it. Mum would be proud.

"Oh, don't be ridiculous," Miss Saunders says bluntly. "I don't hold with pet names, Gloria."

I feel my face flush, and an argument is bursting to escape from my lips. But why bother? I'm sure Miss Saunders is as likely to listen to my request as those horrible children back at the church are to become my best friends.

And so I bite my lip and I head through the

passage to the sitting room, where the steep staircase hides behind the door in the wall.

"Oh, by the way, Gloria..."

Miss Saunders has followed me, and her voice has dipped low, presumably because she's about to say something she doesn't want Rich to hear.

Perhaps she's going to reprimand me for being so forward.

Or perhaps she's got an ultimatum for me. One last chance and then – if Rich has another accident, or we damage her property – we're out.

"I asked Reverend Ashton if he'd heard anything of last night's air raid on London," says Miss Saunders. "Apparently the docks were hit. Your family doesn't live in that part of the city, do they?"

"No!" I reply, my heart flipping with happiness. "Thanks ... thank you, Miss Saunders.

She gives me the briefest nod in reply, and disappears back into the passage.

"Right, now I have a chore for *you*, Richard," I hear her call out, as I blink back tears of relief and begin to clamber up the narrow stairs.

Walking into our room, I see that everything except the upended, still airing mattress has been tidied away. The hatbox is back on its shelf. Clean bedding is neatly stacked on the little cane chair. The spot on the rug where my foot bled is clean and damp from scrubbing.

And most surprising of all, I notice something else: Miss Saunders must have found Rich's spare pyjamas in one of the drawers (I had to push old Mrs Saunders' things to one side to make way for ours).

The stripy pyjamas are laid out on top of the chest of drawers, and on top of *them* is a tiny toy mouse.

Placing the sheet and the potty on the dressing table, I reach down for the mouse. It's hand-knitted and old-fashioned. A toy from Miss Saunders' own childhood, maybe? But what's it doing here?

As I hold the soft toy, I hear voices downstairs in the garden, and go over to the open window.

Miss Saunders and my brother; they're both *inside* the chicken run, somewhere we're forbidden to go.

And Miss Saunders is doing something unexpected; she's pouring chicken feed into Rich's hand, and encouraging him to crouch down and let the hens eat from his palm.

"It tickles!" I hear Rich giggle, as a black hen peck-pecks. He's not scared or nervous or jumpy. Instead he's reaching out a finger to gently stroke the shiny feathers of its neck.

Miss Saunders watches, and doesn't try to stop him.

Has she just let him break one of her rules?

Whatever next? Will she be ordering us to run around the house in muddy shoes?

I don't understand what's happening, but something has changed.

And if it keeps Rich safe and happy, I'm pleased.

Even if *I'm* counting off every second we stay in this stupid village. . .

Making the Best of It?

"Bye, bye, Mr Mousey – be good till I get home from school."

Rich gives the knitted toy mouse a kiss and places it on his pillow.

"It was mine as a child," Miss Saunders told him over tea last night, in her usual tight-lipped, unsmiling way. "But you may keep it, Richard, if it's a comfort, till your mother sends on your, er, Duckie. . ."

Rich went to hug her, but Miss Saunders stood up and took dishes to the sink before he could reach her. Didn't she realize what a compliment that was? No, of course not. . .

"Come on," I call back to him now, as I limp

down the stairs. "I think breakfast must be nearly ready."

I've been hearing the clinking of dishes and cutlery the last few minutes and the smell of newly baked bread has been wafting up to the bedroom as I've hurried to get dressed.

Though my throat feels so tight I'm not sure I'll manage to swallow anything.

School.

That's the problem.

In no time at all I'll have to make my way to the church hall, where the older children are being taught. Lucky Rich; with all the evacuee children in the area, the Thorntree primary school is overcrowded, and the classes have been split so that evacuees attend in the morning and local children after lunch.

That means he'll be back here soon after noon, while I'll have to last for a whole day as the new girl in a room full of staring strangers.

"Everything all right?" asks Miss Saunders, looking up from the bread she's buttering.

"Everything is lovely, Miss Saunders!" says Richard, overtaking me and gambolling to a seat at the table.

But I know the question was aimed more at me than at my brother.

"Yes, thank you, Miss Saunders," I respond with a nod – and thankfully she nods back.

We don't have to embarrass Rich. Miss Saunders only needs to know that we slept well, with no accidents. In fact, Rich loved his exciting trip to the loo in the dark, with the "explorer's" torch to light his way.

"Good, good," says Miss Saunders, as she pops bread on two plates and goes to check on the eggs that are bubbling and boiling in a pot on the range. "Now, Richard, Gloria . . . I just wanted to say that I hadn't expected to end up with two children to look after. Just as I'm sure you hadn't expected to end up staying here with me, I dare say."

She's addressing this speech to the bubbling pot rather than us, so I'm not sure what to say or do except sit down opposite Rich.

"But as it's turned out this way, well, we must think of it as doing our duty. Part of the war effort. We must all just make the best of it."

Behind her back, I frown at Miss Saunders' coolly delivered words. Over the table from me, Rich beams, as if she's been as warm and welcoming as Father Christmas.

"And anyway, even if the roof hadn't been damaged, Mr Wills' farm would have been *quite* unsuitable for you," she carries on, reaching to take a large spoon from an earthenware utensil pot. "I mean, the very idea of placing evacuees in a household with no woman present..."

"It's not the farmer's fault," Rich pipes up. "Mum's friend Vera said his wife die— *passed away*."

"Huh!" snorts Miss Saunders. "Is that the story people are believing? No, no... Mrs Wills ran off *years* ago. And now it's just him, and those boys he lets run wild."

The way she said "him", it's clear that Miss Saunders has no great love for Mr Wills. I know I'm only thirteen, and it's not my place to ask about the mystery of missing wives or what's wrong with the farmer exactly, but at least there's something else I think I can find out and still sound polite.

"I know Harry's the older one," I say, "and there's a younger son called Lawrence. But there was another boy at the farm on Saturday..."

And laughing behind the graveyard wall yesterday, I could add but don't. I'd rather not be reminded.

"A thin sort of boy? Dark hair?" Miss Saunders checks, and I nod. "That'll be the evacuee who's been staying with them this last year. Archie, I think I've heard him called."

So that means the boy with the browny-blond hair must be Lawrence. Archie and Lawrence. Please, *please* don't let me be sitting anywhere near them at school today.

"Now," Miss Saunders carries on, while turning back to the eggs, "to make things more … more *homely*, perhaps you should call me Auntie Sylvia. Would that be all right?"

I'm so taken aback, I don't know what to say for a second. What's surprised me more? That Miss Saunders wants us to call her "auntie", or that she thinks being stuck here could feel "homely"?

Rich doesn't bother speaking either. With a screech of his chair, he's on his feet and rushing to hug her.

Miss Saunders – *Auntie Sylvia?* – stands holding the pot with one hand and the spoon in the other and seems uncertain what to do about the small boy wrapped around her waist.

"Well, I'm glad you approve," she says at last. "Now sit back down at the table, Richard, and let's get you two some breakfast. One egg or two, Gloria?"

"Just one," I reply, sliding into a chair. And then I think about adding something else, just to see what it feels like. But the words "Auntie Sylvia" stick in my throat.

They feel wrong. Peculiar.

In fact, I feel like this whole day might be *very* peculiar indeed...

"Pssst!"

I ignore the noise. I've been ignoring it most of the morning. It happens every time Mr Carmichael turns round and writes something on the board.

"PSSSSST!"

I think it's the girl making the noise this time. I found out her name when register was called; she's Jessica, Jess for short.

Her pals Lawrence and Archie have been guilty of it too, of course. It's like listening to pipes hissing steam all around me.

But I don't react. It's what Mum always said to Rich about the teasing that went on at his school back home: if you react to it, the bullies will keep pestering you. If you ignore them, they may give up and go away, if you're lucky.

Of course, Rich isn't always lucky.

Oh, how is he getting on? I wonder and worry.

When I took Rich to school this morning, he clung to my hand and repeated his "Glory, Glory, Glory!"s, and straight away children were staring at him. The teacher, Miss Montague, didn't seem very kind either. I tried to say that Rich was a bit sensitive, but you could tell she held no truck with such nonsense. She simply reached over and snatched Rich's hand from mine, saying that no one got special treatment from her; everyone was treated in the same, fair way.

"Please be all right, Rich," I mutter now, gripping my slate pencil so tightly my knuckles go white.

And I'm not only worrying about his time in lessons; how will he manage making his own way home to the cottage? Rich has never gone to or from school without either me or Mum holding his hand. I know it's not far, but what if he gets lost? Or falls in the pond? Or bullies bother him?

"Oi!" the girl's voice hisses behind me. "You, *Land of Hope and Glory.*"

Very funny, I think darkly.

The girl's calling me after that old song because I told the teacher that I preferred to be called Glory rather than Gloria when he added me to the register this morning.

"Jess!" Mr Carmichael snaps, catching the girl at it. "Save your songs for the playground, please! Ah, in fact it's lunchtime now. You may all be excused."

With whoops and screeches of chairs, my classmates clatter lids open, taking lunches out of their desks, then hurry outside. I'm in no rush to join them, to sit on my own in some corner or be bothered by that Jess girl and the boys from the farm.

So I play for time, hiding behind the lid of my desk, pretending I'm looking for something. Though all that's in there is the ham sandwich Miss Saunders made me for lunch. (I doubt I'll *ever* be able to think of her as "Auntie Sylvia".)

"You worked very nicely this morning, Glory," Mr Carmichael's voice booms at me all of a sudden. I take the brown paper bag with my sandwich in it and close the desk lid.

"Thank you, sir," I say shyly.

"I'm sure you'll settle in well," he continues, "though I know it can be hard to find your feet when you're new."

"Yes, sir."

Behind Mr Carmichael's mostly bald head, I see that the clock hands are pointing to twelve. Rich will be making his way out of school any minute.

"There are a lot of your sort here," he says matter-of-factly.

Does Mr Carmichael mean evacuees, I wonder?

"But there *is* one girl I would recommend you steer away from, though," he carries on, gazing at me over his half-moon spectacles, "and that's Jess Brennan. She can be very troublesome. And together with Lawrence Wills and Archie Jenkins. . ."

My teacher drifts off, tutting to himself, and thinking of some incident or other that's aggravated him.

"I suppose the girl can't help it, coming from her background," he picks up where he left off. "But let's just say I think she would be a highly unsuitable friend for a nicely behaved girl like yourself. And I *don't* think she's the type of child of whom a lady of Miss Saunders' standing would approve."

"Yes, Mr Carmichael," I murmur.

My cheeks are flushing as I speak. I have no intention of being friends with that Jess girl, but I don't like the way he said "coming from her background". He's one of those people who look down their noses at anyone who comes from London, isn't he? My old classmates who came back after the Phoney War said there were plenty like that in the countryside. And for all I know, Mr Carmichael may have his eye on me, just waiting for me to put a foot wrong...

"Anyway," says Mr Carmichael, slapping his palms on his lap, as if he's about to change the subject, "are you, erm, settling in well with Miss Saunders?"

My teacher's voice has that funny note of doubt and surprise in it that I heard from the shopkeeper on Saturday, when I went to fetch the sugar.

"Yes, thank you, sir."

"Very respectable woman, Miss Saunders. Though she does rather keep herself to herself."

"Yes, sir."

I don't say any more than that, even though I have the feeling that Mr Carmichael would love to find out what goes on behind the closed front door of the village's most private resident.

"Miss Saunders was a fine primary school teacher, you know," he carries on, settling himself on the corner of his table. "A real loss to the profession when she had to give it up. But with her mother being ill and her father long dead, I suppose she had no choice. It's just a pity that the only time we see her is at church, and she was always so very busy and rushing straight home afterwards to her mother ... and now she's busy with *you* chaps, of course."

It's interesting hearing a little more about Miss Saunders. But to be honest, I don't want to be sitting here chit-chatting with my teacher about her or any unsuitable friends I might or might not have. Right now, I happen to be too anxious about Rich to concentrate.

"May I – may I be excused, Mr Carmichael?" I ask, in the most polite voice I can manage.

"Yes, yes, my dear," he says, waving me towards the door. "Enjoy your lunch, get to know some of your classmates, and see you back here in twenty minutes."

Twenty minutes. It's a shorter lunch break than I get at my school back in London, but lots of the kids here live on farms and need to get home as quickly as they can in the afternoon, and help out with work before the light fades.

Anyway, I can easily do what I need to do in twenty minutes.

Racing out of the church hall, still clutching my lunch, I head for the gate. Pulling it open and slipping through, I'm aware of more than one voice yelling out a chorus of "Land of Hope and Glory", but take no notice. Because I know that if I hurry down the lane and get to the green, it's only a short distance to the primary school, and Rich.

And there – *there* he is!

"Rich!" I call out to him, spotting my brother at the end of the lane, crossing it on his way back to the cottage.

"Glory, Glory, Glory!" he calls back as I run to him, only vaguely aware of the stinging pain in my foot as panic overwhelms me.

Something's happened, hasn't it? He isn't smiling. He looks smaller, more like a frightened bird, than when I saw him only three hours ago.

Maybe it's the fact that his socks are rumpled around his ankles, revealing the scatter of pink dots where the blisters have newly healed.

Maybe it's the oversized baggy navy shorts that are flapping around his puny legs.

Wait a minute; *they're* not his shorts. Rich's two pairs – lovingly packed by Mum – are grey, and actually fit him.

"What's going on?" I ask breathlessly as I reach him.

Rich bursts into noisy tears, thudding his head into my chest.

"Hey, hey!" I say, gently placing my hands on either side of his face and kneeling down in front of him. "What's wrong?"

Miss Saunders asks the same question as we tumble through the back door of the cottage a few minutes later.

She's taking a pie out of the oven. I want to grab it from her and run back to Rich's school, where I'll throw it in the face of his Miss Montague!

"Rich was scared of his teacher," I tell Miss Saunders, my heart and head pounding, my hand squeezed tight around my little brother's. "He was too frightened to ask to go to the lavatory, so he. . ."

I hold up the brown paper parcel that I found Rich carrying. There's no lunch in this particular bag – just a soggy pair of grey shorts and underpants.

The fight suddenly goes out of me.

Miss Saunders has a strained look on her face. Have we disappointed her again? Is she disgusted with the news that Rich has had yet another "accident"?

"Dear me," she exhales, placing the pie dish down on the top of the range. "Well, what are you waiting for, Gloria? You must hurry back to school or you'll be late for lessons. *I'll* deal with Richard."

I'll deal with Richard. The words repeat in my head as I reluctantly let go of my brother's hand and back out of the door.

I'll deal with Richard. The words dance around as I stumble back towards the church hall.

"*I'll deal with Richard*," I mumble worriedly as I take the few steps up to the heavy wooden door of the hall and push it open. "What does she mean by that?"

It's only then that I realize the yard behind me is empty, and the makeshift classroom in the hall is full. While I've been fretting, everyone else has filed in and taken their seats.

Thirty or more pairs of eyes fix on me as I make my way to my desk.

Three pairs in particular seem to be watching my every move.

Why are Jess, Archie and Lawrence so interested in me? Can't they just ignore me? I'd like that a lot better.

"Sorry I'm late, Mr Carmichael," I say hurriedly, slipping into my seat.

Someone – a few someones – snigger around me.

"Since it's your first day, I'll let you off, Miss Gilbert," says the teacher, sounding less friendly than he had earlier. "But let this be the last time you're tardy!"

"Yes, sir," I say, quickly lifting the lid of my desk to take out my slate and pencil and—

"*EEEEEEEE!!*"

The scream; it's me.

The bellows of laughter; that's everyone else.

"What on earth!" bellows Mr Carmichael.

He takes two long strides and is by my side, seeing what *I'm* seeing.

The snails, the countless snails oozing inside my desk and covering my slate, seem completely unbothered.

"Who did this!" booms Mr Carmichael. "Own up now or the consequences will be much worse!"

I'm not sure the rest of the class can even hear his words, they're all howling and roaring so much.

All except one person, who's whistling the tune of "Land of Hope and Glory"...

11

Blue Eyes
Red-Rimmed

Four days.

That's how long we've survived school, me and my brother.

I think I've come off best; no one would own up to putting snails in my desk on Monday, so *everyone* got punished, and now no one speaks to me. That's all right; I prefer it like that. In fact, I've made sure it stays that way by being last to arrive in the morning (I hide behind the holly bush till I see everyone making their way into the church hall) and leaving last at the end of the day (Mr Carmichael appreciates my help tidying up).

And lunchtimes are taken up with rushing to meet Rich and delivering him back to the cottage.

Poor Rich.

Every day is the same. The same fear, the same "accident".

Miss Saunders hasn't said much about it, but since that first day she's taken to sending Rich to school with a clean pair of underpants and shorts packed in his satchel, and a paper bag to bring home his wet things.

Every afternoon, I've come back from school, seeing my brother's newly washed clothes drying on a stand in front of the range, ready to be packed in his satchel "just in case".

Now it's Friday, just gone noon, and I'm here at the primary school gates, watching as children bumble out into the arms of waiting mothers (I feel a twinge in my chest).

"Rich!" I call out, seeing him jostled in the middle of a gang of kids who act like he's invisible.

He's pale. White. Blue eyes red-rimmed.

It's happened again.

"It's all right, never mind," I say as Rich reaches me.

Then I see he's got nothing in his hands. No soggy bag for me to take.

"Rich?" I say, brightening. "No accidents today?"

"Can we go?" he pleads, taking my hand.

"Of course," I say, moving away from the mums who are looking him up and down. I haven't a lot of time anyway; I need to find out what's going on, get him home and get myself back to school on time to keep on the right side of Mr Carmichael. "So what happened? Didn't you need to use the loo today?"

"I did! And I showed my teacher the note Auntie Sylvia wrote for me."

Rich takes a scrunched-up piece of paper from his pocket and passes it to me.

Dear Miss Montague,
    As you will know, Richard Gilbert is currently in my charge. As his "guardian", I would request that you give him leave to use the lavatory if he should present you with this note.
    I would greatly appreciate your consideration.
    Yours sincerely,
    Miss S. Saunders

"When did Miss – I mean, Auntie Sylvia give you this?" I ask Rich, startled by Miss Saunders' thoughtfulness. Or perhaps she just didn't want to wash so many clothes.

"When you were out collecting the eggs this morning," he blinks up at me.

His black eye has faded to yellowy-green, his eyebrow is beginning to grow back, he didn't wet himself. This should be a good day, but it clearly isn't.

"So you showed this note to Miss Montague, and she let you go to the loo, right?" I say, running over the facts as we walk past the cabbages and their fluttering white namesakes.

"Right," he mumbles.

"So why are you unhappy?"

Rich immediately bursts into tears.

"Glory, Glory, Glory!" he practically shrieks, slapping his hands over his face and stamping his worn-but-polished boots on the ground.

"What? What is it, Rich?" I stop and ask, my heart racing. He's hysterical. And I know better than anyone that it's very, *very* hard to get through to him once he gets this anxious.

I'm also aware of the prying eyes of school parents *and* the time passing, so all I can do is wrap an arm around him and steer him towards the cottage as quickly as I can.

"Hello, children. The postman brought a parcel for you this morning," says Miss Saunders, glancing up from some darning. Straight away, I spot her looking at my hands for the telltale paper bag, and her surprise when she realizes there isn't one. Then she sees the mess Rich is in. "Dear me, Richard! Gloria – what's happened?"

Hearing her use my full name sets my teeth on edge, but of course it's not the time to challenge her about it.

"Your note worked," I tell her instead, setting my sobbing brother down on a kitchen chair. "But I don't know what's wrong – he won't stop crying."

As I kneel beside Rich, Miss Saunders gets up from the table and crosses to the sink. Quickly, she runs a washrag under the tap, then strides back over to us and begins to dab it on Rich's neck, face and forehead. It works like a charm. The cold cloth seems to bring him to his senses, and the hiccuping sobs subside.

"Now, Richard," says Miss Saunders, pulling up a chair and settling herself down next to him. "There's nothing in this world that can't be sorted. But equally, nothing can be sorted if you don't talk about a problem."

It sounds like something a wise owl would say. Or perhaps a teacher. A nice one, I mean.

"Is it Miss Montague? Did she upset you again?" I ask Rich, as I fish around for what's troubling him.

"I – I did a wrong thing, Auntie Sylvia," says Rich, directing his words to Miss Saunders rather than me.

"What was the wrong thing, Richard?" she asks him in a measured voice, sounding neither cosy nor cross.

Richard takes a shuddering big breath.

"I was feeling a bit lonely, so I – I took Mr Mousey to school today, in my pocket."

Rich bites his lip, tears trembling in his eyes, waiting for the wrath of Miss Saunders.

"Are you trying to say you *lost* him, Richard?" she asks, still in that measured tone of voice.

Not Miss Saunders' childhood toy! My brother wasn't *that* careless, was he?

"No," he says, shaking his head. "I came back from the lav, and I was whispering to Mr Mousey, telling him I did it, I did it! But Miss Montague saw and got very angry and consif – consifitated—"

"Confiscated it?" I help him out.

"Uh-huh," Rich mumbles with a barely there nod. "Are you *very* angry, Auntie Sylvia?"

Miss Saunders stares at my brother, her lips as thin and tight as I've ever seen them.

"Yes, I am, Richard," she announces, standing up and grabbing her jacket from the peg on the back of the kitchen door. "Come on, come with me!"

"What?" I burst out, unsure what's happening. "But Rich didn't mean— I mean, it's not really his fault!"

I'm following Miss Saunders out of the cottage and round the green, babbling apologies and explanations of Rich and his funny little habits and sounding desperate and rambling and scared. Rich is simply white-faced and panic-eyed as he hurries and scurries after us.

"Shush – calm yourselves!" Miss Saunders orders us, as her long strides direct us towards the primary school.

Acting like she owns the place, Miss Saunders shoves open the gate to the playground and swoops through the heavy blue swing doors of the small Victorian building.

Clack-clack-clack go her sensible brown shoes along the corridor. Then she pauses at a classroom door, just long enough to rat-a-tat on the glass panel.

Before anyone inside has a chance to say "Come

in", Miss Saunders places a hand firmly on Rich's back, propelling him into the room ahead of her.

Unsure what I'm meant to do, I follow far enough to hover at the doorway, and see Miss Saunders and my brother standing in front of the teacher's desk. Miss Montague – a sandwich halfway to her mouth – seems shell-shocked at the interruption to her lunch.

"Can I help you?" she asks frostily.

"No – I'm going to help *you*, Miss Montague. I'm going to help you understand something here," Miss Saunders says in a voice so taut it could break. "Have you noticed Richard's legs?"

Miss Montague lets her eyes drop to Rich's skinny calves, the pink blister marks visible – as usual – because of his fallen socks.

"Well, yes," says Miss Montague, her nostrils flaring, as if she's regarding some kind of slum child skin condition with barely hidden disgust. Same as Miss Saunders did on Sunday, when she saw Rich in his bath. The thought of that makes me touch my own ugly, puckered scar on my cheek.

"And this?" says Miss Saunders, pointing to Rich's healing black eye and peculiar, stubbly eyebrow. "Do you know how this happened?"

"I presume he'd been in a fight at his old—"

"And this?" Miss Saunders barges on, pulling up the sleeves of Rich's bottle-green jumper.

His arms are a criss-cross of scratches and burns, some deeper and fiercer than others.

Miss Montague now frowns, sensing something more serious is being shown to her.

"His whole body is covered with injuries like these, Miss Montague, because Richard and his family were caught in a bomb blast. A bomb blast in which someone died. Didn't Reverend Ashton explain that to you when he told you a new evacuee would be joining your class?"

I'm holding my breath, hardly able to believe what I'm hearing. Miss Saunders is totally on Richard's side. She is his champion, riding into battle with the dragon that is Miss Montague.

"Well, Reverend Ashton said something about Richard's home being damaged in a raid, but I didn't realize the black eye and the marks on his legs were injuries or—"

"This young boy – a boy of only *seven* – has been through an experience adults such as ourselves can barely imagine," Miss Saunders carries on regardless. "So I'll thank you to show him a modicum of kindness and understanding from now on, Miss Montague. Starting with the return of his toy mouse, please."

Rich is staring up at Miss Saunders, a little puzzled by what's happening and some of the words she's using, but liking the sound of this last part, I'm sure.

"I – I – didn't realize. If I'd known..." Miss Montague fumbles for words at the same time as she fumbles in her desk, then hands the knitted mouse to my brother.

"Thank you!" Rich gushes, cuddling it close.

"Good day to you," says Miss Saunders, sweeping out of the classroom so quickly I nearly trip over my feet in an effort to get out of the way.

I might be off-balance, but one thing's for sure: I'm *positive* I saw the faintest hint of a smile on Miss Saunders' face as she breezed by me just now...

There's a soft moan, and I quickly switch off the torch.

I stay still as a statue, trying not to rustle the letter in my hand.

Good – his breathing is becoming soft and steady again.

Click.

In the soft yellow torchlight, I watch Rich snuggled up beside me, deep in sleep.

Today, my brother has gone from being the most upset I've ever seen him to the happiest. Right now his tummy is full of apple crumble (double helpings), he's reunited with Duckie (the parcel Miss Saunders mentioned earlier was from Mum), and his old toy and Mr Mousey get on famously. You can tell from the way they're both snuggled in Rich's arms, duck beak smushed up against mouse whiskers.

So it's safe to read again, although I know Mum's short letter off by heart already.

My darling Glory and sweet boy Rich...
Hope this letter finds you well. Dad and I are fine and busy, busy, busy with work.
Guess what: we have new neighbours! A Mr and Mrs Jones have rented Mrs Mann's old flat and very nice they seem too.
Yesterday, we had an unexpected visitor. Mr Taylor popped by yesterday to see the state of his dear old

home ...he and Mrs Taylor are living with relatives till they see what's what. But wouldn't you know it he's planning on rebuilding his chicken coop as soon as he can get his hands on some netting, so we shall expect some squawking around here again!

Anyway, Rich — here is your darling Duckie. I gave him a big kiss to pass on from Dad and me!

Glory — I hope you are looking after your little brother well and being helpful and courteous to Miss Saunders.

And both of you — look out for a big surprise coming your way soon!

Love always,
Mum and Dad xxxx

PS Buttons and Betsy send purrs!

Carefully, I fold the letter, slip it back into its envelope and place it on the table beside me. Clicking the torch off, I rest it down too, then slip oh-so-gently out of bed and pad to the curtained window.

Sleep won't come easily, I'm sure; there's too

much to think about. So all I want to do is lay my head on the cool glass of the windowpane, look out into the inky darkness of the countryside and wonder... Wonder what Mum's big surprise is (food? sweets? clothes?) and wonder at how marvellous Miss Saunders was today. How could I have got her so wrong? It wasn't till I was hurrying back to school that I realized something really important. On Sunday, when I caught her staring at Rich in the bath, it *wasn't* disgust on her face, it was despair. Despair that this skinny little boy – singing happily to himself in the tub – had to bear these wounds of war.

She might not be as free with smiles and hugs as Mum, but after her rant at Rich's teacher earlier, I know that Miss Saunders *does* care – about my brother, at least, which is fine by me.

And as long as Rich is all right, then I can muddle through.

I can put up with living in this silent, polished house with our odd "Auntie Sylvia". Same as I can put up with being shunned at school and—

But what's that?

For the second time in a few minutes, I stay still as a statue, head tilted, listening.

There ... a sound I'd never expected to hear in the cottage.

Music.

I tiptoe across the cold wooden floorboards, the softness of the rug, more floorboards, and find my slippers.

With only the faintest squeak, I open the bedroom door and make my way slowly, slowly down the stairs, my toes feeling for telltale creaks on the way.

The wooden door at the foot of the stairs – it's closed, but a soft glow from the fringed lampshade floods through the cracks.

And the music ... it's the sound of a piano being played as softly as it's possible to play; notes in a tune being slowly picked out.

I know the tune. It's something old-fashioned, from the time of the Great War, I think.

"If you were the only girl in the world, and I was the only boy..." I mouth along to the melody, as I stand on the bottom step and lean against the cold wall.

Hearing music again is so wonderful. It makes me yearn for evenings by the fire at home, the wireless on, Lil flinging her skirts and dancing, Mum singing along while Dad smiles – and Mrs Mann thumps on the ceiling with her stick. Ha!

The laugh catches me out, and I slap my hand across my mouth to contain it. But my elbow catches the door . . . and it swings gently open.

"Gloria!" says Miss Saunders, sitting at the piano and looking as guilty as if I'd caught her sitting there buck-naked and not in a fastened-to-the-neck blue dressing gown.

"Sorry, Miss Saunders!" I gasp, feeling just as caught-out and exposed. "I heard the music . . . it was so pretty!"

Miss Saunders looks like she's about to order me back to bed, then appears to think better of it.

"Come in and shut the door, for goodness' sake, before we wake your brother."

I pad down one final step, shut the door behind me, and wonder what to do with myself. Since I'm still uncertain what Miss Saunders' opinion of me is, I reckon the best option is to stand right next to the piano and take up as little room as possible.

Miss Saunders gazes at me for a second through her wire-rimmed spectacles, and I notice for the first time that her eyes are grey too. Silvery-grey as granite in this light.

She let her wrists sink, but her fingers still rest on the ivory-white and shiny black keys.

"I'm sorry, Gloria," she says finally.

I'm not sure what she's sorry for, so I mumble an awkward "S'all right."

"No, it's not. I haven't been totally … *welcoming* to you this week, and you must forgive me. I really am unused to visitors – over the years we had them so very rarely, my parents and I. Except for the doctor, that is," says Miss Saunders. "And it's been so long since I gave up teaching that I'd quite forgotten how to speak to children."

Shyly, I rub my goose-pimply arms and smile at her, trying to think what to say next. Then I remember that Mum always says that a compliment is like a gift.

"You play well," I tell her.

"Oh, not any more!" Miss Saunders laughs, glancing down at the keys again. "I haven't played this out-of-tune thing for years, Gloria."

"*Please* call me, Glory, Miss Saunders," I say softly, the words tumbling from my mouth before I can stop myself.

Miss Saunders studies me carefully for an unnerving moment or two.

"Very well, *Glory*," she says finally. "But only if you will call me Auntie Sylvia."

I nod, and we smile at each other, which feels nice.

Then Miss Saunders' – *Auntie Sylvia's* – fingers start to move, playing the same song over again, and this time I sing softly along to it.

And this time, I see for certain that Auntie Sylvia is smiling.

Laughing, in fact.

But it's not because of my singing; it's because of something in the now open stairwell doorway – a felt duck and knitted mouse who're waltzing together in Rich's arms...

Sunshine and Shadow

"Oh, this is beautiful," I say.

"The attic?" laughs Auntie Sylvia. "Why, Glory – it's practically a zoological park for spiders up here!"

She stands on the ladder and passes me a box that's packed with her mother's clothes from downstairs. There's another waiting to be handed to me, and two stuffed suitcases are already up here. We really have worked hard together this morning, clearing old Mrs Saunders' things from the bedroom, and other parts of the house as well.

"No, *this*!" I say, shoving the box under the eaves and shuffling along on my knees till I can reach out and run my fingers over a black enamel-painted sewing machine. Curlicues of gold meander their way across it, which is made more obvious now that I'm brushing a woolly layer of dust away.

"You know, I used to make all my own clothes," says Auntie Sylvia with a smile, her head and shoulders poking through the trapdoor. "But, well, Mother didn't like the racket it made, so I told Father he might as well store it up here."

Mrs Saunders Senior must have ruled this cottage and its inhabitants with a rod of iron from her sickbed. But since last night, when Auntie Sylvia played that sweet old-fashioned tune on the piano, it's as if the genie has been let out of its bottle. The whole mood in the house is definitely lighter and brighter this morning.

And while Rich has been busy feeding the hens, introducing them to Duckie and Mr Mousey and going off on an errand to the shop, I've been more than happy to help Auntie Sylvia with her out-of-season spring clean.

"Our flat back in London is on the ground floor, so we don't have an attic," I say, gazing around at the treasure trove of interesting chests and pictures and bric-a-brac. "All that's upstairs from us is another flat, where Mrs Mann used to live... But Mum said in her letter that some very nice new people have moved in."

"Your mother must miss you very much," Auntie Sylvia says quite kindly. "And your father."

I feel a prickle of tears in my eyes at the mention of Mum and Dad.

"And you must miss *your* parents," I say, thinking – with a twinge of yearning – that Mum would be proud of me for that adult and thoughtful comment.

Auntie Sylvia's eyes cloud over a little. "Well, yes, though it was ... difficult at times. Anyway, all this chatter isn't getting these last things moved, is it, Glory?"

She disappears back down the ladder. As I wait for her to lift the last box up, I flick through a pile of old frames next to the sewing machine. Most of them are dark brown and empty of pictures, except for the occasional stained and faded watercolour.

And then there's this one.

"Here!" Auntie Sylvia wheezes, slapping the box up on to the attic floor.

"Miss Saunders—"

"I thought we'd agreed on Auntie Sylvia?" she says, with a faint, hopeful smile.

"Oh, yes!" I laugh shyly at my mistake. "Auntie Sylvia, if you don't mind me asking, who's this?"

I turn the sepia photograph of a handsome young man around towards her. He has a dark moustache, laughing eyes and is wearing a soldier's uniform.

And straight away I wish I'd left it alone.

The smile slips away from Auntie Sylvia's face, and the sunshine feeling of the morning goes with it.

"He was ... well, my sweetheart, Glory. But the war – the *last* war – came between us."

I shouldn't have asked! Here's some young local man who might have married Auntie Sylvia and given her a new surname. She might have had children galore in a happy, noisy house instead of being stuck here in silence looking after her elderly parents. Her beloved must have died in some foreign field, taking all her dreams with him. And now I don't know what to say to make everything better. I've cast a shadow over the nice time we've been having.

"I think I should go and look for Rich – he's been gone a long time," I say, delicately placing the portrait against the eaves.

"Yes. Yes, you probably should, dear," Auntie Sylvia agrees, and backs down the ladder so I can clamber after her and escape.

And outside I run, run, run to the shop, glad of the sudden autumn chill in the air. After her kindness and apologies, the last thing I want to do is upset Auntie Sylvia. So if I can help Rich carry the groceries home from the shop, we can start afresh. I see the way Auntie Sylvia looks at him, in that same adoring way he looks at his Duckie and now Mr Mousey.

But wait . . . the *Closed* sign is on the shop door.

I whip around, looking for Rich on the green, chasing butterflies amongst the cabbages or throwing stones in the pond.

He's not there.

He's nowhere.

"Rich?" I call out.

Where IS he? If I lose him, Mum will never forgive me. Same goes for Auntie Sylvia, I suspect.

"RICH!!"

"Looking for your little brother, are you?" someone calls out.

I glance around and see Jess from school, leading – of all things – a grunting, fat pig out from behind the pub.

"Yes," I answer cautiously, as if I expect her to trip me up with a tease or some meanness. "Have you seen him?"

Jess stares hard at me. Her eyes – a strange pale, glassy green – are small in her pinched face. I can't tell whether she hates me or simply thinks I'm less important than the pig at the end of the rope she's holding.

"He went up Eastfield Farm," she says finally, chucking a thumb over her shoulder, as though Rich and Eastfield Farm couldn't be of less interest to her.

"Why?" I say out loud, but soon realize it's pointless; Jess isn't going to give me a straightforward answer.

Sure enough, all I get is a shrug.

I whirl round and run, leaving Jess to walk her pig who knows where, and head in the direction of the lane and the farm.

It only takes me a couple of minutes to sprint as far as the sign. And as soon as I take the turning, I see the five-bar gate where Lawrence and Archie were sitting staring that first day – and hear boys' voices coming from the messy yard beyond.

I'm too breathless to call out for Rich, but reach the gate and see him anyway.

And what I see makes me gasp.

"What's going on?!" I yelp.

The three of them glance round, and at least

Lawrence and Archie have the decency to look embarrassed.

For some unknown reason, they have brought Rich here and persuaded him to take his clothes off! He's standing there – in the yard – wearing just shorts, boots and socks, with his jumper, shirt and vest piled up on the straw-and-mud-covered ground.

"We ain't – we ain't—" Archie garbles uselessly, his blue eyes staring pleadingly at me like a stray dog that's just stolen someone's dinner.

I realize I've never heard Archie talk at school, only snigger at something either Jess or Lawrence has said or done. Well, if he makes as little sense as this, I don't feel as if I'm missing anything.

"Rich, get your stuff and come here now!" I order my startled brother.

His face whiter-than-white, his eyes filling with panicky tears, Rich does as he's told, scooping up his clothes and scrabbling over to me.

"Hurry!" I hiss at him, helping him over the gate.

"Look, we didn't do—"

"I don't care what you did or didn't do!" I yell over my shoulder at Lawrence as I hurry away, hauling Rich with me by the hand. "Just stay away from my brother!"

That's it.

It doesn't matter how nice and kind Auntie Sylvia has turned out to be, there's no way we can stay in this stupid village with these mean children (and teachers!) a moment longer than we have to.

The minute we get back to the cottage, I'm writing a letter home, telling our parents we need to be rescued. . .

13

The Truth About the Truth

"You and Richard must simply stay away from them," says Auntie Sylvia, taking her long strides towards church this Sunday morning, her head held high.

She keeps her gaze directly ahead, catching no one's eye, as if she's got blinkers on, same as a racehorse.

"Those boys are no good," she adds. "The whole family is no good."

I told Auntie Sylvia something about Lawrence and Archie yesterday, but not all of it.

I told her I'd caught them teasing Rich, but ended it there.

I *meant* to say more; I'd planned on ratting the

boys out, hoping she'd go storming up to Eastfield Farm and give them and Mr Wills a piece of her mind, same as she'd done with Miss Montague at the school. But when me and Rich got back to the cottage, we'd found her sitting staring at the sheet music on the piano, her hands in her lap, not playing.

It was my fault, of course. I'd reminded Auntie Sylvia of her long-ago love, the boy snatched away by war. And suddenly it didn't seem right to make her angry as well as sad.

"Richard, *please* keep up, dear," Auntie Sylvia turns to say. Rich gives up his sulky stone-kicking and hop-skips to her side, clutching Duckie and Mr Mousey.

At the same time, he gives me a hurt puppy look, knowing I'm cross with him but not really understanding why.

"I was only showing them my chest!" he'd said yesterday when I hurried him back to the cottage.

"Well, that's not for strangers to see," I'd said briskly, bundling him back into his vest, shirt and jumper. "And anyway, those boys are silly and just want to laugh at you. All right?"

"But, Glory—"

"You don't have to understand," I practically snapped at him, I was so cross. "You just have to do as I say, Rich."

Of course, my brother isn't used to me talking that way, which is why he's acting upset and wary with me now.

And Auntie Sylvia might be upset with me too, if she knew what the letter in my hand actually said...

"Is it all right if I go and post this?" I ask Auntie Sylvia, holding up the stamped envelope.

Last night she dared to try the wireless, and was delighted to find it still worked. So while we listened to a show, Rich read one of his old comics, Auntie Sylvia darned, and I wrote to Mum and Dad with my "news". News that secretly contained the "come get us" plea.

Because comfy as we are at the cottage, I know I need to protect my brother from mean and hurtful people, like those awful boys at the farm.

"Yes, certainly," says Auntie Sylvia. "Richard – can you stay with your sister? I want a quick word with Reverend Ashton before the service starts."

With that, she hurries around the green towards the church, while Rich and I take a shortcut through the cabbages to reach the postbox outside the grocer's shop.

But now I wish we hadn't – I've just spotted Jess sitting with her back to the oak tree, as the pig she seems to be in charge of crunches at acorns scattered on the ground.

"Hello!" Rich says brightly to her.

"Hello to you, Titchy-Rich!" says the girl.

Titchy Rich? She has a *nickname* for my brother? I didn't even know she knew what his first name *was*. That suddenly makes me mad. She has no right to act like she knows him so well!

"Come on," I order my brother.

"Hee hee!" I hear him giggle. "I'm Titchy-Rich! Titchy-Rich!"

"Rich – let's go," I hiss at him as I walk off towards the red postbox.

"No, I want to say hello to the pig. Why do you have a pig?"

"It belongs to Charlie and Mary, who own the pub," I hear Jess say, while I keep walking. "It lives round the back."

"Can I stroke him, please?"

Why isn't Rich doing what I tell him? He *always* listens to me.

"Sure. His name's Popeye," Jess tells him. "Here..."

As I cross the road, I turn to see Jess scramble to her feet, and pass the pig's ropelike lead to my brother.

Oh, no ... with that done, Jess starts walking towards me. What does she want?

"Oi, Hope 'n' Glory!" she calls out, just loud enough for me to hear but not Rich. "What were you playing at with Lawrence and Archie yesterday?"

"What do you mean?" I ask, trying to stand as tall as Auntie Sylvia, and adopting her tight-lipped owl glare. I hope Jess can't see that I'm shaking like a jelly inside.

"I mean, yelling at them like they'd kidnapped your brother," she snaps, her birdlike dark eyes flashing menacingly. "It wasn't *their* fault he came up to the farm – the shopkeeper sent him up there. He'd run out of chicken feed and told Rich he could buy some from the Willses!"

I didn't know that. Rich didn't tell me. But that doesn't change what they did when he got there.

"They didn't have to egg him on to take his clothes off and make a fool of him!" I snap back, as I fidget with the letter I'm still holding in my hand.

Oh, no. Over Jess's shoulder I can see Lawrence and Archie walking with Mr Wills and Harry in the direction of the church. And now the two younger boys have split off and are ambling our way. Lawrence is walking tall, a broad, cheeky grin on his face. Archie shuffles at his side, keeping his head down and peering over at me through the mop of dark, straight hair falling over his forehead.

"They did *not* egg him on!" Jess barks at me. "They asked Rich about what it was like living in London with air raids. Next thing, he's pulling off his shirt, trying to show them the scars he got when you lot got bombed."

Oh.

I wince, which makes my own spider-legged scar tug at the skin on my cheek. The thing is, I *could* imagine Rich doing exactly that; trusting people a little too easily, and then taking it too far.

"Well, fine . . . but they didn't have to be cruel and laugh, did they?" I point out, noticing that the boys have stopped to talk to Rich and the pig.

Jess turns to see what I'm looking at.

"Hey, Lawrence! Archie! Did you two laugh at Titchy-Rich yesterday?" she bellows at her mates.

"No!" Lawrence calls out, echoed by – of all people – *Rich*.

Archie just frowns, like he wants to shout something pretty rude at me but is holding himself back.

I quickly remind myself of what happened in the farmyard ... and my tummy gives a lurch of embarrassment. They're right; I heard boys' voices, but no laughter.

"I tried telling him not to take his stuff off," Lawrence calls out, pointing his finger at my grinning brother, who's now *hugging* the pig. "I said he'd catch his death of cold!"

"I – I just thought—"

"You just thought the worst of them, didn't you?" Jess sneers in my face, putting her hands on her hips. "Just like all the snobs in this village."

"Jess!" Lawrence suddenly calls out, but his friend is in the middle of losing her temper with me, and is enjoying herself too much to stop.

"*Specially* that snooty Miss Saunders you live with."

"Jess!"

"*She's* the worst, always looking down her nose at all of us!"

I can't get a word in edgeways, Jess is raging so.

It's as if her voice is a roar in my ears.

Only it's not.

The roar is something else.

I look up into the sky and see the dark shape of a plane against the blue sky.

It's low; way, *way* too low, skimming the treetops, looming over the village.

I can make out the face of the German pilot inside, or his white teeth, at least, bared in fear at the prospect of crashing, or—

THUNK!

Out of nowhere, Archie does a rugby tackle on me and Jess, his skinny body hitting us surprisingly hard. The three of us crumple into the recessed doorway of the grocer's shop in a tangle of arms, legs and gasped "oof!"s – just as the rat-a-tat-a-tat of strafing machine-gun bullets pepper the dirt road where we were standing just now.

And as soon as it happens it's over, with the whine of the plane passing overhead.

For a few stunned moments we three are in limbo. I feel Jess's body shaking in shock under my arm, and the weight of Archie half-sprawled across us both, his chest heaving as he tries to catch his breath.

Then there's a sound: a dull thunk coming from the direction of the fields that are part of Mr Wills' land.

"It – it – it's crashed!" Archie stammers in shock, scrabbling to his feet.

"The pilot; he was trying to *hit* us!" I say, gratefully taking the hand that Archie is holding out to me. "Didn't he see we were just kids?"

As I say the last word, the blood drains from my face.

"Rich. Rich! RICH!!" I yelp, shaking myself loose from Archie's grasp and running over to the green.

I can see no one.

There's only Popeye the pig, bucking and squealing, panicked and trying to free itself from the rope that's holding it.

"Lawrence?" Jess is screaming, running alongside me.

We see Lawrence first, his head rising up from the cabbage patch.

"Where's Rich? Where is he?!" I demand, bounding through the cabbages towards him.

"Here," Lawrence replies, woozily getting to his knees – and I see that he must've thrown himself on top of my brother.

I reach to help an equally woozy Rich to his feet, Duckie and Mr Mousey peeking out of his pockets, while Archie and Jess put their arms around Lawrence and lift him up.

You know, when I first stepped off the bus in this spot, I thought Thorntree was unnaturally quiet.

But now there seem to be people everywhere, streaming out of the churchyard and running and shouting in the direction of either us or the fields of Eastfield Farm.

"Yay! Popeye's all right!" Rich cheers, before the stampede reaches us. "I held on hard as I could to keep him safe!"

He lifts a small hand to show the rope wrapped tightly around it.

I'd expected to find my brother shaking, a victim once again of the Nazis, but instead he's smiling like a hero...

14

A Change of Plan

Auntie Sylvia's tin of Epsom salts is coming in handy again.

She's made a salve for the various burns on Rich's hands.

One is his hero burn, from the rope he had wound tightly around one hand to keep Popeye from running off and into danger.

The others are stupidity burns. They're dotted on his fingertips, where he picked molten-hot bullets from the road to keep as mementos.

Rich seems to think the stupidity burns were worth it; he's staring at the row of dark metal bullets laid out on the kitchen table as if they're precious jewels. Duckie and Mr Mousey are standing guard over them.

"My, my, will you look at that," says Reverend Ashton, examining Rich's injuries. "But you're a strong little lad, Richard, and I'm sure those will heal in no time!"

The vicar has come to check on us after this morning's drama.

And to let us know what happened to the plane – and its crew.

"So, the plane landed in the Wills' wheat field rather than in the cattle fields?" Auntie Sylvia comments as she nurses, displaying an impressive knowledge of Eastfield Farm. "Lucky for the cows, I'd say."

"And lucky for the crewmen that the field had just been ploughed," adds Reverend Ashton. "They parachuted out seconds before the plane came down."

"Quite the soft landing," Auntie Sylvia comments, now winding a bandage round one of Rich's hands.

"Yes, though it's just as well I got to them at the same time as Harry Wills and the other young men," Reverend Ashton adds with a wry smile, "or the airmen's welcome might have been a *lot* more painful, what with the pitchforks and spades the lads were waving around!"

"Would they have hurt the pilot and his friends?" Rich asks, alarmed.

"Um, no . . . no, they wouldn't, I'm sure," Auntie Sylvia says quickly, to stop my brother from fretting. "They just had them as a precaution, in case the German pilot or his crew were armed."

"Will they lock them up in the Tower of London?" asks Rich, his blue eyes wide at the prospect. "And put them in chains?"

"No. The police will arrange for them to be taken to a prisoner-of-war camp, Richard," Auntie Sylvia explains. "They'll be treated fairly and allowed to write letters home to their mothers, through the Red Cross, I expect."

Suddenly, I remember the letter in my pocket, unsent and now crushed.

I'll post it later; if Thorntree is now just as dangerous as London, we might as well be back *there* with our parents.

"And you're not to worry yourself, young Richard," says Reverend Ashton, about to give my brother a reassuring pat of the hand, till he thinks better of it. "I spoke to the military police, and they say this is a complete one-off. This pilot fellow was *way* off course, *miles* from where he should've been."

Rich blinks at Reverend Ashton, hanging on his every word.

"The squadron he was part of dropped their bombs in the early hours and then headed back to base. So you see, our little corner of England is still the best, safest place for you to be. The same can't be said for those poor souls down in Lond—"

Auntie Sylvia looks as horrified as I feel hearing those words. Luckily, she dives right in before the vicar blurts out how bad things are at home and frightens the living daylights out of Rich.

"Thank you very much for coming to tell us the news," she says while getting to her feet, which forces a comfy and surprised Reverend Ashton to do the same. "We won't keep you. You must have so much to do!"

As Auntie Sylvia holds the back door open for the vicar, my head buzzes with thoughts of home, anxious to know the state of my city, and more importantly, my little patch of it. (Oh, I hope this raid wasn't on our doorstep!)

"Now, I think we've had quite enough excitement for one day," says Auntie Sylvia, coming back and settling herself down to bandage Rich's other hand. "But would anyone like to hear some more cheerful news?"

"Yes, I'm sure we would, wouldn't we, Rich?" I answer for both of us.

Rich nods enthusiastically.

"Well, for the last few weeks Reverend Ashton has been rather *pestering* me about something. Two things, actually," Auntie Sylvia begins.

I think of last Sunday, when she sent us off to the common, on our doomed damson hunt. Sure enough, she didn't exactly look as if she was about to engage in an enjoyable conversation with the vicar. If fact, she looked so tight-lipped and serious, I'd thought she was going to talk to him about sending us away.

"You see, Miss Montague has enlisted in the WAAF—"

"What's that?" Rich interrupts, patiently holding his hand in the air while Auntie Sylvia pops a safety pin into the bandage to hold it in place.

"Women's Auxilliary Air Force," I tell him. It immediately makes me think of Lil in the Land Army, and I feel a pang of longing for my dizzy-headed sister.

"Exactly. Anyway, for the last few weeks, Reverend Ashton has been trying to persuade me to take over her role as organist."

"You're going to play the organ in church?" I ask, amazed at the idea of Auntie Sylvia being brave enough to place herself publicly on view to the villagers.

"Yes, yes I am. Reverend Ashton says it's my duty not to waste the talents I've been given, such as they are," Auntie Sylvia continues. "But more importantly, Reverend Ashton has asked me repeatedly to come out of retirement and teach in Miss Montague's place. I have to confess, I've been very much against the idea up till now. But as a certain young man is a pupil at Thorntree School, I rather thought it might be something I should reconsider."

She's smiling kindly at my brother, who hasn't a clue what she's saying.

"You mean, you've decided to be Rich's teacher?" I double-check.

"Well, yes, that's what I wanted to tell Reverend Ashton before church this morn—"

She doesn't get to finish her sentence.

Rich suddenly understands, and he reaches over and throws himself around her neck, wrapping Auntie Sylvia in a grateful cuddle before she can do anything about it.

"Well!" she says, uncertain what to do with her

own hands and holding them uselessly in the air. "I take it you're pleased with the news, Richard?"

"Oh, yes, yes I am!" I hear his muffled response.

Auntie Sylvia locks eyes with mine, and I see hers are twinkling behind the glass of her spectacles.

"Jolly good," she mutters softly, and lets her arms settle stiffly across my brother's back.

So Auntie Sylvia cares enough about Rich to become the teacher at his school.

Rich can hardly believe his good luck.

The bombing in London is still bad.

Things here aren't perfect, but these three reasons mean I'll be tearing up my letter to Mum and Dad and throwing it on the fire. And then I'll write them a new one.

Dear Mum and Dad,
    Rich and I are very happy and having a lovely time with Miss Saunders, who we now call Auntie Sylvia...

15

The Wrong Friends

"...and of course, I don't suppose you have much of a chance to see beauties like *this* in London!" says Mr Carmichael.

He's talking about a newt.

It's wriggling about in a glass jam jar that Mr Carmichael dipped in the stream just now on our "nature" excursion.

I want to tell him that we do, actually, because there's a river close by where we live in London, and then there's the big fishing pond at Alexandra Palace. And on day trips to the Lea Valley with school we get to see all sorts of wildlife.

But thinking about that has reminded me of all my old classmates and everything familiar and I feel a sudden, sharp pang of homesickness in my chest...

"Mmm" is all I manage to mutter to my teacher instead.

"Now *this*, of course, is the palmate newt, which people often muddle up with the common newt because of... Hey, Johnny! Leave that bird nest alone and come down from that tree this instant!"

Thank goodness for Johnny.

Since no one in class talks to me, I've ended up walking and talking all morning with Mr Carmichael, and it's become a little tiring. I mean, his knowledge of the hedgerows and berries and birds is very interesting, but he *has* tried to turn the conversation to Auntie Sylvia every now and then – "Is she taking good care of you, especially after yesterday's near-miss with the plane?" – and I don't feel comfortable being a tattletale. Yes, the whole village might wonder what she's like behind closed doors, but Auntie Sylvia's been too kind to Rich, to both of us, for me to betray her trust.

So now I'm glad I can just sit here in peace for a few minutes and eat my sandwich, while Mr Carmichael is busy yelling at Johnny, who seems to have got himself stuck halfway up an oak tree.

"Who's your friend?" a voice asks.

It's Lawrence. He sits down next to me, brushing his fair hair back off his face, and I notice that his eyes look the goldy-brown of syrup in this light.

"Huh?" I mumble, through a mouthful of cheese sandwich. I feel shy and stupid; I don't know what he's on about.

"What's his name?" Lawrence carries on, with a grin. He's nodding down at the jam jar that Mr Carmichael left behind.

"Ha! His name's Bob," I find myself joking, plucking a random name from the air for my "friend" the newt.

"Well, hello, Bob – nice to meet you!" Lawrence jokes back, lifting the jar to inspect the wriggling creature at close quarters. "Hmm? What's that you say, Bob?"

He puts the jar to his ear, pretending to listen to something. I can't help giggling.

"You want to get back home? Your wife's got the dinner on? Fair enough!"

And with that, Lawrence leans forward and pours the newt and the tea-coloured water back into the stream.

"Oh!" I gasp. "Won't you get into trouble for doing that?"

I'm pleased he did – the poor newt wasn't having the best time trapped in the jar – but Mr Carmichael might go as mad at Lawrence as he was with Johnny just now.

Lawrence glances over his shoulder, then lays the jar on its side.

"I'll say I kicked it over by accident when I came over here to ask you how you are," he says, turning his beam of a smile in my direction. "So how are you? And how's your brother?"

"I'm fine," I tell him, still feeling a little shy. "And Rich is fine too. Well, he burned his fingers on those bullets he picked up and had to wear salve and bandages on his hands all day yesterday."

Rich quite enjoyed the novelty of his bandaged hands, and having me feed him his lunch and tea like a baby. He even came out with a disappointed "Aw!" when Auntie Sylvia unwound them this morning before they set off for school together.

"Snap!" says Lawrence, pulling a dented bullet out of one pocket and holding up the fingers of his other hand so I can see the blisters on his thumb and forefinger.

I can't help laughing, but then immediately sober up when I remember I owe Lawrence something. An apology.

"I'm sorry I didn't get a chance to say thanks, for protecting Rich, I mean. Everything got so busy when all the people came running. . ."

"S'all right," says Lawrence. "I thought it would be easier to shield him than Popeye. He's a *lot* smaller."

Lawrence is funny. I thought he was just annoying – along with Jess and Archie, he was probably responsible for the snails in my desk after all – but he is actually funny. And I owe him a *second* apology.

"And sorry . . . for shouting at you up at the farm," I say sheepishly. "I thought you were teasing Rich. A lot of people do."

Even Jess, I think, remembering that day she was egging Rich on to jump at the butterflies and mimicking what he was saying.

Lawrence stops grinning and just nods, playing around with a blade of grass in his fingers.

"Well, I wouldn't do that. Your brother's a nice kid. Better than a lot of the kids in this place. . ."

He sounds bitter. I'm not sure what to say, so I don't say anything.

"You getting on all right here? In the village?" Lawrence asks, turning the conversation back to me.

"Um, it's fine, I suppose. It's just ... well, the people in Thorntree aren't very friendly."

The words are out of my mouth before I know it. I hadn't meant to say that to Lawrence at all, especially since – until yesterday – I thought about *him* as one of those unfriendly people.

"Ha!" Lawrence laughs out loud. "You're not exactly friendly yourself, you know, Glory Gilbert!"

"*Me?*" I say in surprise.

"You should have seen the look you gave me and Archie that first day you walked up the lane to the farm," he says, with his cheek-to-cheek grin. "Your mum was looking at this bit of paper, Rich was just sort of hopping around the way he does – and you ... you just looked straight at me and Archie and gave us this *scowl*."

He pulls a face that's part frown, part glower, part ridiculous. It would be funny if it wasn't an impression of me.

"It was like you *hated* me and Archie without even knowing us!"

"I didn't mean to do that," I say hurriedly. "I was just nervous and not sure what to expect. . ."

"Well, maybe you do it because you're nervous, but it makes you look like you want everyone to keep a million miles away from you. You might as well just growl!"

"Is … is that the way I seem to everyone?" I ask Lawrence, stunned, and thinking of how my classmates steer clear of me.

"Well, yes," he replies with a so-what shrug. "We thought you were as stand-offish and snooty as Miss Saunders."

There it is again, the fact that people don't really like Auntie Sylvia. . .

"But most of the people at school aren't worth knowing anyway," Lawrence carries on, twiddling the blade of grass in his fingers. "The locals all stick together, the evacuees all stick together, and then there's me, Archie and Jess, and none of 'em bother with *us* at all."

He's right; I might not know my classmates very well, but I can see there's a big divide between the locals and Londoners. And sure enough, none of them talk to Lawrence and his friends.

"Why? I mean, why don't they bother with you?" I ask him, pushing aside my shyness now that curiosity has got the better of me.

Lawrence splits the blade of grass with his fingernail, and seems to be thinking; thinking if he'll tell me, if he can trust me, maybe.

"Right, then!" Mr Carmichael shouts out. "Now that Johnny has kindly deigned to get down from the tree, let's continue with our educative walk, girls and boys! And no, we are NOT going to go and look at the crash site again, so don't keep asking!"

Lawrence is on his feet before me, and I presume he's going to head off and find Archie and Jess ... but he doesn't.

As I start walking, he falls into step beside me.

Mr Carmichael hesitates, as if he's waiting for me to catch up with him, then frowns when he sees that I've made a friend.

And from my teacher's expression, he seems to think Lawrence is the *wrong* sort of friend for me to have. . .

"What's wrong with his face? Looks like he's chewing a wasp!" says Jess, looking back at the church hall, where Mr Carmichael is standing in the doorway, his eyes on us all and deep lines furrowing his forehead.

"I think he's wondering why I'm not staying to help tidy up today," I tell her.

"Why *aren't* you staying to help, Hope 'n' Glory?" she asks bluntly, as we all go through the gate out on to the lane.

"I'm just a bit tired," I say, coming out with a little white lie.

It's too complicated to explain that I want to know how Rich got on with Miss Montague. Auntie Sylvia took him down to school this morning and was going to pick him up at lunchtime, "so there's no nonsense," she said sniffily. I love the fact that Auntie Sylvia wants to keep an eye on my brother. And I'm sure she also wanted to look around the school with fresh eyes, now she's decided to take over Miss Montague's class shortly.

"Me too," says Jess, swinging her battered satchel back and forth. "Didn't get to bed till late 'cause of having to help out in the pub."

Mr Carmichael is still watching us, I notice. He clearly wasn't impressed with Lawrence hanging around with me today on our nature walk, and he looks even *less* impressed with the company I'm keeping right now. To be honest, I'm not really sure why Jess, Archie and Lawrence waited for me in the yard after school today. Perhaps Lawrence has told them that I'm . . . all right?

But do *I* feel all right about hanging around with *them*?

I don't know much about Archie since he never talks – he just stares a lot with those puppy-dog eyes. As for Jess, well, she still scares me a bit. Quite a lot, actually.

"Er, aren't pubs closed on a Sunday?" I ask Jess, as the thought suddenly occurs to me.

"Yeah, but sometimes Charlie the landlord has some friends round, for a *private* drink," she says with a wink. "And the place was lively last night, with everyone talking about the plane! I was cleaning glasses till all hours."

I feel a twinge of pity for Jess, having to work till late last night, when all I'd had to do was cuddle up in Auntie Sylvia's comfy spare bed with Rich and his toys.

"Hey, remember that pub on the corner back home, Archie?" Jess turns and asks the other boy. "That place was mad on a Friday night! What was it called again? The Lamb and what?"

"The L-L-Lamb and F-F-Flag," Archie stutters his reply.

I'm so unused to hearing his voice that it's always a surprise to hear how soft and low it is compared to Lawrence's confident boom.

"They were evacuated together," Lawrence tells me now, while Jess gabbles some story about the rowdy-sounding Lamb and Flag and she and Archie fall around laughing behind us. "They went to the same school in the East End of London."

"Oh! I didn't realize the two of them knew each other before they came to Thorntree," I say as we walk ahead together.

I also had no idea that Archie had an actual stammer. When the plane came at us, I thought he was just stuttering in shock. But if he has a real, actual stammer . . . that must be the reason why he never answers a question in class, or talks out loud in front of everyone.

"So Jess and Archie have been in Thorntree over a year?" I ask, keen to know more.

"Uh-huh," says Lawrence, lazily kicking at a stone in the road and sending it flying. "And when they were evacuated, the rest of their school got billeted in Basildon, except for them."

"What do you mean? Why didn't they stay in Basildon too?" I ask.

"They didn't get picked by anyone there," Lawrence says with a shrug. "The evacuation officer had to scramble around half the villages in

Essex trying to persuade someone to take the two of them in."

"Oh, how awful," I reply. "But *why* didn't they get picked?"

"Well, Archie won't talk to anyone he doesn't know, 'cause of his stammer, so people thought something was wrong with him," Lawrence says matter-of-factly. "And Jess – she's just a bit mouthy, isn't she? You can imagine how well *that* went down!"

"You talking about me, Florence?" Jess bursts in, jumping on Lawrence's back.

"Oi – don't call me that!" Lawrence laughs, trying to wriggle her off him, but she hangs on so tight he ends up giving her a piggyback. "Anyway, I was just telling Glory why you two ended up here on your own."

At his words, Jess stops grinning and flops her head on Lawrence's shoulder. She shoots me a sideways glance.

"I miss my lot," she says, almost softly. "Got three brothers and a sister in Basildon. Only seen them once since we got here. But then I haven't seen the two little ones at all; they're back in London with my mum and dad."

"There are seven of you?" I gasp at the size of her family. "There are only three of us, and that's bad enough."

Of course it's not bad at all, even when Lil takes over the dressing table with all her things and keeps dropping her hairpins on the floor for me to stand on in bare feet. . .

"It's like I've got two brothers: Harry and you," says Lawrence, turning to grin at Archie. They're obviously the best of best buddies for him to say that.

"So have you got brothers – *real* ones, I mean – Archie?" I ask him.

"N-n-no. It's just me and my m-m-mum. Haven't s-s-seen her in a year."

Archie is blushing as he speaks, as if he's shy of letting me hear his voice.

"I hope my parents come to visit us soon," I say wistfully. "But I don't know when I'll see my sister, Lil, again. She's in the Land Army."

"What – she *chose* to work with pigs and digging and stuff?" Jess sniggers. "I mean, Popeye's quite sweet, but cleaning up after him ... urgh! If I was older, *I'd* join up proper. Be a WAAF. See a bit of action."

"You'd be stuck at a desk, serving tea to the

officers, you mean!" Lawrence teases her, and runs off at a gallop with Jess giggling on his back.

Which leaves me and Archie dawdling on our own together.

"Hey, G-Glory, did you know that on S-S-Saturday night, there's a film sh-showing in the ch-church hall?" Archie suddenly says enthusiastically.

"Really?" I reply.

I *am* interested; that sounds fun. But I'm also slightly preoccupied with watching Lawrence and Jess gallop and yelp their way closer to the cottage. I hope Auntie Sylvia doesn't look out and see who's making all the noise.

"Uh-huh. I don't know what f-f-film they'll be showing yet. But the fish and chip van is coming to the village too. See?"

Archie points at a chalkboard sign saying as much, leaning up against the side of the pub. But I can't concentrate on reading the board or listening properly to what Archie is saying because Lawrence has come to a stop *right* in front of the cottage, and Jess is waving madly at us to hurry over and see something.

"I'd better find out what's going on," I say to Archie, and break into a run.

He follows me, and we arrive beside Lawrence and Jess, who each have a forefinger pressed to their lips.

They're staring through the cottage window, watching as tall, grey owl Auntie Sylvia waltzes – awkwardly – with my seven-year-old brother. I can hear some scratchy old tune being played.

"Ppppffffff!" Jess snorts, which sets Lawrence off.

"Shush!" I whisper, trying to shut them up.

But it's too late.

Auntie Sylvia turns and frowns at us all.

"B-b-bye!" says Archie, as he, Lawrence and Jess scuttle away before the front door is thrown open.

"What's going on, Glory?" Auntie Sylvia demands, looking along the road at the fast-retreating figures of my friends.

"Nothing! I was just walking home with them and—"

"Inside, please."

Her voice is stern. I think she is either cross with me, cross with Lawrence, Jess and Archie, or cross with herself for being spotted doing something frivolous.

"Look, Glory!" Rich chatters excitedly as the door clicks shut. "Auntie Sylvia got the gramophone to

176

work. And she was showing me how her dad taught her to dance when she was a little girl!"

"Now, dear, I really don't want you hanging around with those children," Auntie Sylvia says to me, crossing her arms and ignoring Rich completely. "They're really not very nice."

"Oh, but I didn't think they were very nice either," I try to explain, "till they helped save me and Rich yesterday."

"They didn't 'save' you, Glory," Auntie Sylvia corrects me in quite a stern, teacherly voice. "You were all just in the same place at the same time, and very lucky to escape serious harm."

"Glory, Glory, Glory?" mumbles Rich, coming to slip his hand into mine. He doesn't like the heated way we're talking to each other.

"It's fine, Rich," I say, giving his hand a squeeze.

Because of him, I'm not going to argue with Auntie Sylvia, but I feel suddenly so frustrated and confused. Why is *everything* so muddled in this village? Why is Auntie Sylvia being so unfair and unkind about Lawrence and the others? She doesn't seem to want to believe that Archie was brave enough to put himself in danger to push me and Jess out of harm's way. And Lawrence did the same for Rich.

On the other hand, why are my new friends – and lots of other people in Thorntree – not particularly nice about Auntie Sylvia?

"Glory's right, Richard. Everything is fine," she says, trying to regain her composure. "Now, how about a glass of milk and a—"

Clonk-clonk-clonk!

We all stop dead at the sound of the rarely used brass fox door knocker.

"Who on earth can that be?" Auntie Sylvia wonders aloud, astounded that anyone should be there, since visitors are so very rare at the cottage.

While she pauses for a second and tidies her hair behind her ears, I take the opportunity to peek out of the window.

"Oh!" I gasp, getting goose pimples.

For there, on the doorstep, stands the big surprise Mum wrote about in her letter. . .

16

The Unexpected Visitor

The girl on the doorstep is wearing a green sweater, deer brown jodphurs and chunky lace-up boots.

She's also wearing a slick of red lipstick, a high-rolled hairdo that must have taken a lot of time and effort to do, and far too much perfume. I could smell it practically before Auntie Sylvia opened the door. It reminds me a little of the scent of the sweet factory, wafting over our whole neighbourhood back home.

"Can I help you?" says Auntie Sylvia, clearly wondering who this rather flashy young woman is.

"Lil!" Rich yelps.

He ducks under Auntie Sylvia's arm and rushes at her.

"Hey, Squirt!" Lil laughs, hugging and tickling him at the same time. "Miss me, did you?"

"It's Lillian, our sister," I tell a visibly flummoxed Auntie Sylvia.

"Oh, oh, I see. Do come in, then, Miss Gilbert!"

"Miss Gilbert? Oh, no – that's too posh for me," Lil laughs. "Plain Lil will do nicely, ta."

"Well, do come in, *Lillian*," says Auntie Sylvia, sounding a little uncomfortable with the sudden familiarity.

"What are you doing here?" I ask my sister, too stunned to know what to do or how to act. It's just so bizarre to see her here in Auntie Sylvia's little sitting room.

"Oh, shut up and give me a hug first!" Lil says in her usual straight-talking way, and holds an arm out for me.

I rush to her, suddenly thinking of home and us, giggling together in our bedroom about some nonsense or other.

"Oh, Lil..." I sigh, burying my face into the scratchy wool of her jumper.

I can't help it. I sob and sob and sob, while she hugs me tight, kisses my head and tells me it'll be all right.

"Wish I could've come and seen you all after what happened," she murmurs, "but Mum wrote and said not to bother; that everyone was fine, and anyway, she was sending you and Rich here to Thorntree as soon as she could."

I cry more, the memories of the plane yesterday and the blast back at home crushing and pushing to the front of my mind, even though I've been doing my best to keep them locked away for my brother's sake, so I can be strong for him.

And then I feel Rich wriggle his hand into mine and know I have to pull myself together.

"I'm fine, Rich," I tell him, breaking away from Lil's comforting cuddle.

I'm expecting to see worry etched on his face, but instead he's smiling.

"I know," says Rich, patting my hand. "And Auntie Sylvia says to come through to the kitchen – she's making tea and says we can have biscuits!"

That makes me laugh – and cry too, with sheer relief. I don't have to shoulder the responsibility for looking after Rich all by myself. Auntie Sylvia is looking out for him, and now Lil is here too, even if it's just for a quick visit. I didn't realize how much I just wanted to be a thirteen-year-old girl, instead of a grown-up in charge of a small boy, gorgeous as he is...

"Come on then, Rich," Lil says cheerfully, as she links her arm into mine. "Lead the way!"

We go through the passage and into the kitchen, where Auntie Sylvia is laying the table, using the best china that I've only seen out when Reverend Ashton has been here.

"Mm, smashing!" says Lil, bowling right up to the table and helping herself to a home-made piece of shortbread. She screeches out a chair and plonks herself down, quite at home.

Me and Rich sit down too, but wait till Auntie Sylvia passes us the plate before we take our shortbread.

"So, Lillian ... what brings you here?" Auntie Sylvia asks, now pouring tea into the dainty china cups. She's glancing warily at my sister, unsure if she likes her manners, I worry.

"Well," says Lil, talking with her mouth full, "I'm finished my training with the Land Army now—"

"Was it fun?" Rich interrupts.

"No! It was not!" Lil laughs loudly. "It's hard work, Squirt. Look at my hands! And my nails! Thank God I can still do my hair and wear lipstick, or I'd look like a *complete* country bumpkin. Ha!"

I feel like shushing her. Doesn't Lil realize that could seem like slur on Auntie Sylvia, who lives here in a little village – in the country?

"So, are you on your way to a farm?" I ask her, hoping Lil will answer me and talk normally, more politely.

I don't want Auntie Sylvia to get the wrong impression of her. Though it's probably too late for that already. . .

"You bet!" Lil says with a grin, taking out a mirror compact and checking her lipstick for crumbs. "Me and my chum Sally were all set to be sent to this *awful*-sounding place. Get this: it was halfway up a hill, miles from anywhere, with only a farmer's wife for company. Not a handsome man in sight – ha!"

She snaps shut her mirror compact case.

"So me and Sally said no thank you very much to *that*. And then I'm talking to the officer in charge about other farms looking for help, and – *ta-nah!* – here I am!"

"What do you mean?" I ask her.

"Me and Sally; we're only working up the road from here – at Eastfield Farm!"

"Yay!" yells Rich, jumping off his seat to hug Lil.

Meanwhile my head is reeling at the surprise. And I spot Auntie Sylvia flinch at the mention of Eastfield Farm, as if she's been slapped.

"Well, I . . . I . . . do you think that's appropriate?" she asks Lil. "I mean, Mr Wills has no wife. You girls will be quite unchaperoned."

"Ha!" Lil laughs in Auntie Sylvia's face, as if that's the silliest thing she's ever heard. "Me and Sally don't need chaperoned, love. We'll manage very well, don't you worry."

My toes curl at hearing Lil call Auntie Sylvia "love". What is she doing? I love Lil. I'm so pleased she's here. But I wish she'd shut up. She's gone from comforting me to *embarrassing* me in just a few minutes flat.

"But how can you stay at the farm, Lil?" frets Rich. "*We* couldn't. They have a broken roof and not enough bedrooms."

"Don't you worry, Squirt," says Lil, ruffling Rich's hair till it's messy. "Me and Sally are in Mr Wills' son's room. Do you know Harry? The oldest one? He's bunking down in the hayloft."

"We've, um, met him," I tell her. I glance quickly across at Auntie Sylvia and see that her lips are pursed into that tight line she does when she's disapproving or agitated. She's probably remembering the last time she spoke to Harry, when he was haranguing her on the doorstep, trying to get her to take us in.

"Well, how lovely for your brother and sister to have you so close," says Auntie Sylvia, remembering her manners, even if Lil hasn't. "Will you stay and have dinner with us, Lillian?"

"No, ta!" says Lil, getting to her feet and grabbing herself another shortbread biscuit. "Mr Wills is expecting me back. Got to unpack and get a tour of the farm with Sally."

"Perhaps you might come and eat with us on Saturday, then?" Auntie Sylvia suggests instead. "About six o'clock?"

"Oh, yes, please. Say yes!" Rich begs Lil, jumping up and down as she walks towards the front door, scattering crumbs in her wake.

"Yes – great. See you then. Ta ta!"

With kisses blown, Lil leaves in a fug of sugar-sweet perfume – and leaves Auntie Sylvia with a distinctly cold expression on her face.

And me? I'm left feeling cross with Lil for being almost cheeky to Auntie Sylvia.

But I'm cross with Auntie Sylvia too, for looking

at Lil as if she's the most common girl she's ever set eyes on.

Thank goodness for my darling Rich, I think, wrapping an arm around him.

He may be odd, but he's the most straightforward person in this muddlesome world I'm now living in. . .

17

Shush, Don't Tell

"She's good fun, your sister," says Lawrence.

"Yeah, she's *r-r-really* good f-fun!" Archie joins in.

I'm feeling muddled again.

Me and Rich have come to the common to have a walk and muck about with Lawrence, Archie and Jess. I couldn't wait to get here.

But now I'm irritated and a bit jealous. Lil came to see us on Monday, and now it's Thursday. I know she's coming for dinner on Saturday, but it's hard hearing what fun someone *else* is having with your sister in the meantime.

"What's wrong with *you*, Hope 'n' Glory?" asks Jess, spotting something's up.

Not that I'm going to tell her; Rich is missing Lil madly now that she's so close but yet so far.

"I'm all right," I say, as I stroll and watch Rich skip-hop in zigzags through the long grass just ahead of us. "Just a bit tired."

That much is true. I sat till late at the bedroom window last night, my eyes fixed on the faint orange glow on the dark horizon, my nails digging in my palm as I watched London burning again, knowing there was absolutely nothing I could do except keep my fingers tightly crossed that it hadn't affected Mum and Dad.

"You've got a face on you, that's all," Jess comments, putting her own face uncomfortably close to mine.

I'm still a little scared of Jess. In their different ways, I like easy-going Lawrence and shy and sweet Archie a lot now that I know them better. But Jess. . .

"Leave Glory alone," Lawrence tells Jess now, seeing my predicament and wrapping an arm around her neck in a jokey stranglehold.

"Get off!" she yelps, but looks like she's loving it.

Actually, does she sort of *like* Lawrence, I wonder? But then I think probably not. Jess just might be the most fearless and tomboyish girl I've ever met. I bet she'd think I was having a laugh if I suggested she liked Lawrence any more than Archie, or Popeye the pig, even.

"So are you g-g-going to see the film Saturday, G-G-Glory?" Archie suddenly asks me.

His cheeks are a little pink when he talks. I bet if boy-mad Lil was here, she would think he was about to ask me out. Ha!

"Yeah, come," Jess says to me as she wriggles free from Lawrence's grasp. "It's a Western. Yee-ha! Stick 'em up, pardner!"

She acts like she has guns in her hands – Lawrence and Archie both grin and put their hands in the air. Rich turns to see what's going on and starts neighing, pretending he's on a horse.

"I don't think we can come. I don't think Auntie Sylvia would approve," I tell them all.

Another ripple of muddle engulfs me.

I lied to Auntie Sylvia earlier, saying me and Rich would come here and gather her some damsons at last – and missed out the fact that we were meeting Lawrence, Archie and Jess.

"Ooh, *her*! She wouldn't approve of anything that's fun, would she?" says Jess, now putting on a la-di-dah pretend posh voice. "Probably thinks going to see a film is too common, the silly snob that she is."

"She's not *really* a snob," I try to say in Auntie Sylvia's defence. "It's more that she's a bit shy, I think."

"Ha!" snorts Lawrence. "Pull the other one! When I was little, I remember that my dad used to try to say hello to her in church, but she just ignored him, like he was dirt. So he never bothers nowadays."

Now I'm muddled again. Who's right and who's wrong here? Is Auntie Sylvia more snobby than shy?

"I don't think she has a lot of spare money for things like films," I say instead, though I don't know what Auntie Sylvia's situation actually is.

"But Dad gave us those sixpences, remember, Glory?" Rich stops skip-hopping long enough to say. "Couldn't we tell Auntie Sylvia we can pay for ourselves?"

"I don't think so," I try to let him down gently. In truth, I think Auntie Sylvia has more of a problem with being so close to the people of the village than the cost of tickets.

Maybe she *is* a snob. . .

"Anyway, we've got Lil coming for tea on

Saturday, haven't we, Rich?" I say, as I remember another reason we can't see the Western.

My brother's expression instantly flips from disappointment to joy.

"Hey, Titchy-Rich," Jess suddenly calls out to him. "Race you to that fence over there. Loser's a smelly cowpat!"

"No! I'm going to win!" Rich giggles and hurtles off ahead of her.

Jess muddles me too. One minute she's spiky, the next she's sweet.

"She likes your brother a lot," says Lawrence, nodding after Jess as she speeds to catch up with Rich.

"She didn't always," I can't help myself saying. "The day we arrived, I was in the shop, and when I came out, she was teasing Rich."

Lawrence and Archie swap disbelieving looks and frowns.

"You s-s-sure, Glory?" Archie checks with me.

"I remember Jess telling us about that day," says Lawrence. "She said she was just playing around with him. He was chasing the butterflies, wasn't he?"

I nod, remembering.

"Jess said he was cute, and reminded her of her

kid brother, Tommy. Sort of . . . *different* from the rest of her brothers and sisters."

"T-T-Tommy's her f-f-favourite," adds Archie.

So, Jess has a brother who's a bit like Rich?

Now I'm more muddled than ever.

I got it wrong, didn't I? Same as I was wrong about what happened in the farmyard the day Rich went up there. Jess doesn't just like Rich, she might be one of the few people who actually understands him. . .

"Hey, want to go and see your sister, Glory?" Lawrence suddenly asks, brown eyes twinkling. "She's working in the back field with Harry today. We can take a shortcut if we go over there, through the sprouts."

He might be talking about something silly and smelly as sprouts, but it's as if Lawrence has suddenly offered me a gift.

"Yes, please!" I say, grinning so wide I feel the tug of the scar on my cheek.

"Let's go, then," he says, and breaks into a run, following the direction Rich and Jess ran in. "Last one's a cowpat!"

And so I run and laugh, and forget to feel muddled.

*

"Well, this is certainly easier with someone here to help," says Auntie Sylvia, unravelling a man's knitted blue pullover and wrapping the wool around my hands. "Thank you, Glory."

"That's all right," I say, sitting on the footstool in front of her. "I do this for Mum sometimes too."

The sitting room is very cosy this evening. Auntie Sylvia has lit a fire, and Rich is lying in front of it reading one of his comics and humming along to the song on the wireless.

"Your mother won't mind me knitting a jumper for Richard, will she?" Auntie Sylvia asks.

"No, of course not," I reply, surprised that she's thinking that way.

"Oh, good. I don't want Mrs Gilbert thinking I'm, you know, trying to take over from her. It's just that this wool is so very nice, and since my father doesn't exactly need his pullover any more. . ."

"Did he pass away a long time ago?" I ask softly, hoping my question won't upset her.

"Oh, a long time ago, Glory! I was only twenty-one when he had a heart attack."

I realize now, in the soft, warm light, that Auntie Sylvia must be around the same age as my parents.

I used to think she was older, but it's just because of the sober, old-fashioned way she dresses.

"He was a lovely man, but I didn't see much of him when I was growing up," Auntie Sylvia says, staring down at the wool as she talks. "He was the manager of a bank in Basildon, and worked very long hours. Even at weekends he'd often be at the writing desk here, working away. So I had to be a good girl and stay quiet for him!"

She nods to herself as she recalls her childhood.

"But he looked after me and Mother very well," she continues. "He made some investments, so when Mother took ill and I had to give up teaching, there was enough money for us to live on. Not a fortune, mind you. I won't be buying a fur coat and new hat any time soon!"

Auntie Sylvia is gently joking – I've never heard her do that before. It suits her. Her whole face changes, softens, when she smiles.

Which makes me feel terrible all over again for sneaking off to meet my friends this afternoon. And I didn't much like the way Harry snorted at the very mention of Auntie Sylvia's name when we caught up with him and Lil in the back field this afternoon. "Sitting down to dinner with stuffy Saunders?" he'd laughed when Rich checked that Lil remembered her invitation on Saturday. "I'd rather eat with the cows!"

And I hated swearing Rich to secrecy, telling him on the way home to pretend we bumped into Lawrence and the others by accident. He'd nibbled on the raw Brussels sprout he'd plucked from a towering stalk of them in the field and asked me why he had to shush and not tell about twenty times...

Suddenly, I dip my head down, so Auntie Sylvia doesn't see the guilt written all over my face.

"You must miss them," I say chattily, hoping to continue the conversation and banish my bad thoughts.

"I . . . I . . . suppose I do," Auntie Sylvia says after a moment's silence. "Although it wasn't always easy. My mother was quite a difficult person. She was, you might say, a bit of a tyrant at times."

I think back to the moment in the attic a few days ago, when it occurred to me how lonely life sounded for Auntie Sylvia. If only it could've been different for her. If only she could have married the boy in the picture...

"Your, um, soldier sweetheart," I begin, hoping

what I'm about to say won't sound too forward. "Did your parents like him?"

"Oh, my goodness, *no*. Far from it," says Auntie Sylvia. "Not that it came to anything, obviously, because of the war. Which is something they were very glad of, I'm sure."

She's quiet and thoughtful for a few seconds, and I worry that I've made her sad.

I'm even more positive of that when she stands up quickly, putting the knitting on the armchair, and leaves the room, muttering something about being back in a minute.

"Is she getting us some supper?" Rich says hopefully, glancing up from his comic.

Auntie Sylvia has taken to bringing us buttered toast and a mug of hot milk at this time in the evening.

"Maybe..." I reply, but I can hear noises that don't sound much like supper sounds. There's a clunk of a cupboard door, a rattle of something, and now Auntie Sylvia's brown shoes are clack-clacking back through the passage towards us.

"Here!" she says, holding up a large pottery jar.

I think I'm as confused as Rich.

"I keep pennies in here," she says, sitting back

down on the chair and unclipping the lid. "Spare change for treats and the like."

She spills all the coins out on the small table by her side, and Rich immediately jumps up at the clatter and comes to investigate.

"Only I never spend it on treats. I usually just wait till it's full and take it to the bank whenever I'm in Basildon."

I blink at her, still unsure what she's saying.

"Can we spend it on treats now?" Rich asks with his usual well-meant bluntness.

"Yes! Yes, I rather think we should, Richard," Auntie Sylvia beams. "Why don't we celebrate my new job with fish and chips when your sister comes for dinner? I spotted the sign saying the van is coming to the village on Saturday."

Rich jumps to his feet, whoops, and does a happy little dance to the song playing on the wireless.

"*You Are My Sunshine*. . ." he sings along merrily, out of tune as usual.

Auntie Sylvia breaks into a smile of delight, and begins to clap along as he dances and sings.

I do the same, but even as my brother twirls and jigs, my mind is drifting elsewhere ... to the photo of the soldier in the attic, his dark eyes twinkling with life and laughter, just like Lawrence's.

A thought drifts into my mind.

What must it be like to be in love?

18

The Outsiders

"Can I go on my own? Can I?" asks Rich, pointing at the long, winding queue snaking along the road.

People stand in it, chattering excitedly, holding the newspapers they've brought from home to wrap their fish and chips in.

Lawrence, Archie and Jess have already got theirs and are sprawled together under the oak tree on the green. If my brother is happy to buy our tea, it'll give me a few precious minutes to sit and chat with them.

"Of course. Here," I say, passing the purse to Rich.

Auntie Sylvia's never gone to the fish and chip van in all the years it's been coming, she said, and she's not about to go now. Instead, she's at home, laying the table and buttering the bread, all ready for Lil's arrival.

"What, snobby Saunders let you buy chips, Hope 'n' Glory?" says Jess as I tuck my skirt under me and sit on the cold, hard earth next to her and the boys.

"Seems so," I say, taking a hot chip from the wrap she's holding out to me.

"Are you allowed to come to see the film later too?" Lawrence asks, in a hopeful sort of way.

"No – Lil's coming, remember?" I say.

"Aww," he moans, sounding disappointed. I know he's only fooling around, but I still feel strangely pleased.

"Hey, g-g-guess what's happening *next* Saturday, Glory?" says Archie. His bright blue eyes are sparkling with a secret.

"What?" I ask, blowing on my chip to cool it down.

"My m-m-mum's coming to visit! F-f-first time I've seen her in for ever!"

"That's great," I say, really pleased for him. It's been hardly any time at all since I've seen Mum and Dad but already it seems like for ever. I can't imagine what it's like for Archie, never seeing his mother since the beginning of the war.

Then I sneak a look at Lawrence, who can't have seen his mum in *years*. Will he tell me about her sometime? Maybe when we're alone?

"Here, look at this," Archie carries on, reaching into the pocket of his long grey shorts.

He pulls out a small dog-eared photo of a very glamorous-looking woman sitting on the knee of a grinning man with a moustache, her arm wrapped around his shoulder. She has her head tilted back in a laugh and is kicking up her long legs in front of her.

"Are these your parents?" I ask him, taking in the woman's high heels, swept-up hair and heavy make-up. Lil would swoon with envy.

"J-just my mum. That's her b-boyfriend," Archie says, frowning now. "Or at least it was the one b-b-before last."

I don't know what to say to that, so I pay his mother a compliment instead.

"She's very, er, good-looking."

"Isn't she?" he says, brightening again. "Gorgeous as any H-Hollywood movie star. Wait till everyone here s-s-sees her. *Then* they'll be sorry."

"Who'll be sorry for what?" I ask, confused.

"When we first arrived here, everyone teased

Archie about his stammer," Jess answers for him. "Same as they teased me about my clothes."

She holds up her tartan skirt, and I can see that the material is even more threadbare than I thought. I suppose there's not a lot of money to go round in a family of seven, living in the East End.

"You're lucky you've only had a year of it, Jess," Lawrence laughs wryly. "Everyone round here has always looked down their noses at me and my family, 'cause of my mother running off..."

After he says that there's an awkward silence for a second. Do Jess and Archie know more of this story? Or is it just another of Thorntree's muddles and mysteries?

"Hey, you do realize that no one in the village is going to talk to you either, Hope 'n' Glory," Jess suddenly bursts out cheerfully. "Not now you're *our* friend."

"You're one of the outsiders," says Archie, managing not to stumble over his words for once.

"Hey, The Outsiders! Sounds like the gang in a Western film, doesn't it?" Lawrence points out, cheering up.

"Hold on – I have an idea," Jess suddenly announces. She lays her chips down and fiddles with something on her skirt. It's a kilt pin. "Right, thumbs up, everyone."

"What? What's happening?" I ask warily, as Jess brandishes the sharp pin.

"We're a gang. The Outsiders," she says. "So we should make an oath to each other and be blood brothers. Everyone hold up your thumbs!"

"No way!" yelps Lawrence, waving the kilt pin away.

Archie backs away, laughing and shaking his head.

"Stop being so soft," Jess sneers at both boys. "I don't see Hope 'n' Glory making a fuss. She's survived a bomb. She's made of tough stuff."

I blush at Jess's compliment and go to touch my ugly scar, my reminder of that day. But in truth I'm just as horrified at the idea of taking a blood oath. Some of the boys did it my street once. Little Jack Wilkins must have got dirt in his cut because I remember his thumb swelling up to the size of a *plum* the next day, and it was the same colour as one too.

"Chickens!" mutters Jess, giving up and putting her pin back in her skirt.

"But we can *still* take an oath," I suggest, holding my thumb out to the others.

Lawrence grins, understanding my meaning. He leans in, touching his thumb against mine.

"The Outsiders!" he announces.

Archie and Jess see what we're doing and join in, till our four thumbs press together.

"The Outsiders!" they call out.

"And we press thumbs together as our signal, every time we meet from now on," says Jess, getting back into the spirit of it. "Deal?"

"It's a deal!" I say to her suggestion, and Archie echoes me.

Strangely, Lawrence doesn't.

It seems he's been distracted by someone coming towards us.

"Hello, boys," says a very pretty red-haired young woman. She's wearing the same Land Girl outfit Lil had on and is holding a steaming newsprint bundle, fresh from the fish and chip van.

"Hello, Sally," Lawrence answers. Archie gives her a nod and a wave.

"Which one of your little girlfriends is Glory?"

I feel Jess bristle beside me, horrified at being called anyone's little girlfriend.

"*I'm* Glory," I tell her.

"Oh, you don't look much like your sister,"

laughs the pretty girl, as she tears the paper apart to get at her chips. "Anyway, I've got a message from your Lil. She says sorry . . . she can't come to dinner at yours tonight. We've got too much work to do up at the farm."

She's telling me this with a smirk on her face, as if she's quite enjoying giving me the bad news. I don't much like this new friend of Lil's.

I'm half-aware too of Lawrence and Archie swapping what looks like puzzled glances, but don't get much time to dwell on that, since Rich is now weaving his way through the cabbages towards us, clutching his own newspaper package.

"Glory! I did it, look!" he yelps excitedly.

"I have to go," I say hurriedly as I get up to meet my brother.

He's going to fall to pieces when I tell him that Lil's not coming, and I'd rather that happened well away from the prying eyes of the village. . .

Auntie Sylvia is doing her best to stare straight ahead at the screen, even though nothing is on it yet, as the church hall is still filling up.

She's acutely aware that for most of the people already here, she's as good as a newsreel. *There was shock today in the village of Thorntree when resident Miss Sylvia Saunders came to a village event for the first time in living memory...*

"What did you say this film is called, Glory?" she asks me.

"*Kit Carson*," I tell her. "It's about a cowboy helping lead a wagon train in pioneering times."

"It's got Red Indians in it!" Rich joins in excitedly.

He's been wildly excited for the last hour, ever since Auntie Sylvia heard the news about Lil and went off to get her jar full of change. At the time, he'd been crying so much it took him a minute to hear what she was telling him; we were going to see the film. *All* of us. Auntie Sylvia included this time, since we couldn't go on our own in the blackout.

"Red Indians indeed," Auntie Sylvia mutters, as if she's never heard of anything so frivolous. I just smile and think I could hug her right now, for giving Rich such a lovely treat.

"Auntie Sylvia, they're doing lemonades at a table over there," says Rich, now wriggling around in his seat and staring at the back of the hall, where our school desks have been piled up. "Can we have one? Can we?"

"Rich!" I shush him. "Auntie Sylvia's already paid

for fish and chips and coming here tonight. Don't be so greedy."

"Here..." says Auntie Sylvia, surprising me by passing me her little purse. "Go and fetch one for yourself and Richard. And I may as well have one too."

Her face is stern, and her lips are in their familiar tight line, but underneath I think Auntie Sylvia is quite looking forward to the lights dipping, and sitting in the darkness watching a film.

"I'll come!" Rich pipes up.

"No, you will not," says Auntie Sylvia, grabbing on to his arm as I get up to leave. I don't think she wants to be left on her own...

As I squeeze past groups of people filing in, trying to find enough seats together or just standing chatting, I spot Jess on the far side, sitting with a woman who must be Mary the pub landlady. She gives me a wave, looking pleased and surprised to see me here. There's no sign of Lawrence or Archie yet, but they did say they were coming.

"Can I have three lemonades?" I ask the lady behind the table, and count out the correct money from the purse.

Balancing the three cups in my hand, I carefully turn – and nearly bump straight into someone.

"Oops, sorry, sweetheart!" says a familiar voice.

I glance up – and come face to face with Lil.

"What are *you* doing here?" I ask, frowning at her.

"What a welcome, eh, Harry?" Lil laughs nervously, turning to gaze into the face of Lawrence's big brother, who's standing right behind her. "Look, sorry I couldn't come for dinner tonight, Glory."

"It's *my* fault," Harry says, holding his hands up to show he's guilty. "I had to deliver something in the next village this afternoon, so I asked your sister to come with me, and we went to a tea shop, and then a pub –"

A pub? My sister was in a pub?

"– and now we're here. So *I'll* take the blame, not Lil."

Harry is grinning. Lil is giggling girlishly. I'm so cross with her for choosing a boy over me and Rich that I could throw this lemonade all over her.

"Ladies and gentlemen, could you take your seats, please!" Reverend Ashton calls out. "The film will be starting in two minutes."

"Excuse me," I say flatly and swan past my self-centred sister.

"I'll come soon – I promise," she calls after me.

"I'll catch you at the end of the film and we can talk about it."

Red rage clouds my eyes as I walk back to my seat, and it takes a second to see where Auntie Sylvia and Rich are ... and then I spot them. The row of mismatching chairs looks different now that some other people have shuffled into our row.

"Excuse me," I repeat myself, and realize that the three people now standing to let me get through are Archie, Mr Wills and Lawrence.

Archie smiles, Mr Wills awkwardly touches his cap, and Lawrence whispers, "Didn't expect to see you here, Glory!" as I squeeze by him.

"Glory – look! It's your friends!" Rich yelps, as I reach past Auntie Sylvia to pass him his cup of lemonade.

"Quiet, Richard," Auntie Sylvia admonishes him. "And those boys are not her friends; they're simply her classmates."

If only she knew...

"Here's yours, Auntie Sylvia," I say, passing her a cup and sitting down in the free seat between her and Lawrence.

I notice her hand trembles as she takes the cup from me.

"Are you all right?" I ask in a low voice, knowing that no one will hear us in the hubbub of people excitedly settling themselves.

"Yes, thank you, dear," she whispers back. "I'm just a little startled to have *that man* sit so near me."

"That man"; she must be referring to Mr Wills. I wonder why she dislikes him so much? Enough to make her tremble with . . . with what? Rage? Fear?

But whatever the problem is between Auntie Sylvia and Mr Wills, at least she won't have to see him. Reverend Ashton has just flicked the lights off and expectant "Ooh!"s and "Aah!"s fill the room as the screen flickers into life.

"Hey, you forgot something," I hear Lawrence mutter in my ear, his breath warm on my skin.

In the dark, I feel his hand lift mine, and his thumb press against my thumb.

He holds it there for what feels like a moment too long, and I pull my hand away quickly, feeling strangely shy and unsettled. . .

19

Little Miss Popular

"Pow-pow! Take that, injun! Aaarghh! Pow-pow!"

"I think I prefer it when you're the cowboy's *horse*, Richard," says Auntie Sylvia, gently placing a hand on my brother's shoulder. "The gunslinger is rather noisy for church, don't you think?"

She moves off to her seat behind the organ and I slide into the nearby pew, while Rich gallops in beside me.

"Neigh!" he says, a touch too loudly.

"Shush!" I tell him.

Same as last night, people are shuffling into the rows, taking their seats, though of course this morning we're waiting for Reverend Ashton's Sunday service to begin, not a rip-roaring western adventure.

"Sorry," says Rich, and instead begins to amuse himself by drumming his hands on a hymn book to make the sound of horses' hooves.

"Richard," Auntie Sylvia calls out, beckoning him to her. "How would you like to have a very important job? Would you like to turn my music for me?"

Rich acts like he's been given the biggest bar of chocolate in the world, and goes whooping up to join Auntie Sylvia at the organ.

And now I'm left in the pew, feeling slightly alone and self-conscious.

A burst of laughter makes me jump, and I turn to see several people silhouetted against the doorway of the church. It's Lil – Lil and Sally, standing with Mr Wills, Lawrence, Archie and Reverend Ashton. Lil and Sally are the ones laughing, clapping their hands together excitedly as the vicar shakes hands with Mr Wills, seemingly thanking him for something.

What's happening?

Again, I feel a ripple of irritation at my big sister. She's only just arrived here in Thorntree, and yet Lil's already made herself quite at home. She's even making heads turn; the congregation are staring and smiling at her and Sally as they file in, as if they're rare birds of paradise.

I slink down in my lonely pew, hoping she doesn't see me, but it doesn't work.

"All on your ownsome?" Lil says brightly, walking over and plonking herself down beside me. "What have you done to send everyone away? You don't smell *that* bad."

She stops smiling at her own joke and her hand comes up to touch my face.

"Poor Glory. . ." she says, her finger stroking the puckered red scar on my cheek. "I could give you some make-up to help cover that, you know."

I dip away from her hand and feel my cheeks flush. I hadn't thought about my scar in ages, and now my gorgeous, popular, perfect-looking sister has to point it out.

"Welcome, welcome, everyone!" booms Reverend Ashton from the pulpit. "Now today, before we begin, I have some rather exciting news."

A hubbub of anticipation ripples through the church.

"It seems that up and down the country, communities are hosting fundraising events, to pay for additional Spitfire planes to be built for our brave RAF pilots and crews."

More chit-chat rumbles around the old building.

"And we here in Thorntree are going to host our very *own* event – a barn dance next Saturday!"

Cheers and applause break out, as if we were back in the church hall last night, watching *The End* roll up on screen.

"Now, we have a couple of people to thank for this happening. First of all, a new member of our congregation, who brought the Spitfire fundraising endeavour to my attention –"

Reverend Ashton pauses to hold his hand out towards the pew I'm sitting in – and Lil gives him a wiggle of her fingers in return!

"– and as well as the lovely Miss Lillian Gilbert, we must thank Mr Joseph Wills, who has agreed to have this event take place in his barn."

I lean back and look round for Lawrence's dad, and see him holding his cap to his chest and looking embarrassed at the attention.

"And on that cheerful note, let us sing!" says the vicar, nodding at Auntie Sylvia to start playing.

Buoyed with excitement, voices boom all around, louder than in the previous Sundays I've been here.

"It'll be fun, won't it?" Lil leans over and whispers in my ear.

Not for me, it won't, I think to myself.

There's no way Miss Saunders will let us go anywhere near the barn or Eastfield Farm in a million years. . .

"It'll be fun, won't it?" says Lawrence, echoing Lil's very words from earlier, even though he doesn't realize it.

I glance back through the tangle of tree branches and ivy, ready to run to Auntie Sylvia when she finishes her conversation with Reverend Ashton and comes out of the church. I don't want her to catch me talking to my friends.

And another reason I'm here is that I don't want to talk to Lil. I'm cross with her for pointing out my stupid scar and not having dinner with us last night and being surrounded right now by half the village, all simply *dying* to talk to her about the Spitfire fundraiser and how Little Miss Popular came to hear about it.

Through narrowed eyes I watch her in the middle of the throng, chatting brightly with her arms around Rich, as though she's the most wonderful, caring sister in the world. . .

"I bet Harry's got a Sunday-best shirt he's outgrown." Lawrence continues talking about the barn dance. "Maybe he'll have two – so we both'll look smart, eh, Arch?"

"It'd be b-b-better than this," Archie laughs, showing us the worn and frayed cuffs on his current shirt.

"Well, how do you like *my* party clothes?" Jess jokes, pointing at the tired and badly fitting jumper and kilt she nearly always wears.

"Maybe Charlie and Mary will buy you something new," Lawrence suggests.

"And maybe I'm Cinderella and one of those cabbages on the green will turn into a carriage," she says with a playful snarl on her face.

"Have you got a party dress, then, Glory?" Lawrence asks me, holding my gaze just a second too long and making me think about our thumbs touching in the darkened hall last night. . .

"No," I answer him quickly, hoping I'm not blushing. "Anyway, I don't suppose we'll be going."

Because Auntie Sylvia doesn't like your father, I don't say out loud.

"Of *course* you have to come!" says Lawrence, looking crestfallen. "It won't be the same if you're not—"

"Glory? *Glory!*"

"I've got to go," I mumble, hearing Auntie Sylvia call my name.

I hurry over to her, brushing my hair back into place where the tree branches messed it up as I ran, and hope I don't look too discombobulated.

But I'm surprised to see that Auntie Sylvia is looking rather discombobulated herself.

"Well!" she says, with cheeks that are surprisingly pink. "It seems that I'll be requiring your brother's services as my page turner at the barn dance next Saturday. . ."

"We're going?" I practically squeak in surprise.

"Just for a short while," she explains, trying to tuck her wavy hair behind her ears. "Reverend Ashton has persuaded me that it really is my civic duty to play some uplifting, patriotic music on the piano, to raise spirits."

I feel my own spirits rising, as I realize I won't miss out on the party after all. Though how I can be with my friends – especially Lawrence – without her noticing, I'll have to figure out later.

"Miss Saunders," a man's voice interrupts us, and we both turn to see Mr Wills tipping his cap our way as he hurries by.

Auntie Sylvia's face darkens.

I wonder why the farmer, of all the villagers, bothers her the most.

But that's one question I think might be *too* impolite to ask...

I tried very hard to say no. Honest I did.

But Lawrence, Jess and Archie just wouldn't listen.

"What do you think? Am I a Roman emperor, or what?" says Lawrence, draping a length of the white parachute silk around him. "You lot had better say yes, or I'll have you all thrown to the lions."

"Take it off – don't mess everything up," I tell him, making a grab for the cloth. Auntie Sylvia let me store it – Lil's useless present – up here in the attic.

"Snobby Saunders is in Basildon," says Jess, crawling across the floor to investigate a battered suitcase full of old-lady underwear. "She can't see us, Hope 'n' Glory."

Auntie Sylvia taught in school for the first time

today, and Rich stayed with her the whole time, through the lessons with both evacuees and locals. And then they both went straight to the bus stop and headed for town and the music shop there. Auntie Sylvia wanted to buy new sheet music for the upcoming barn dance, she said.

My job was to come up to the loft and rummage for more clothes to turn into bunting. We made a start yesterday, bumping the heavy sewing machine down the ladder steps and then lifting it one more flight down to the sitting room.

It's now perched on Auntie Sylvia's father's writing desk with a pile of fabric triangles beside it, ready to be stitched on to lengths of rope.

And I'm not only looking through the old clothes up there for possible pieces of decoration. Auntie Sylvia says she'll make some new, smart things for me and Rich to wear on Saturday.

She'll think I'm here on my own, maybe setting aside an old pair of trousers of her father's to cut down into shorts for Rich, or an old crêpe de Chine dress of her mother's to make me a pretty blouse.

But instead, I'm with my friends, who persuaded me to let them "help", though they're actually just mucking around and driving me crazy.

"Now I'm an Egyptian mummy … *woo!*" says Lawrence, throwing the end of the sheet of parachute silk around his face and shuffling on his knees towards me with his arms outstretched.

I duck away from him, feeling shy – and worried. Auntie Sylvia and Rich won't be back for at least another hour, I think, but it's going to take me for ever to tidy up the mess that my friends are making.

"What about this?" says Jess. "Does it give me an hourglass figure?"

Lawrence bursts out laughing before I can see what our friend's doing, so I know it's going to be bad.

It is.

Jess is holding an oversized, boned, pink corset around her waist. Old Mrs Saunders must have been a big woman, totally different from her tall, slim daughter.

"Take it off," I say, though I can't help giggling.

"Look at all this s-s-stuff!" says Archie, who's flipping through the picture frames leaning against the walls. "My mum and me, we don't have 'stuff'. Our f-f-flat's too small."

Archie's getting really excited about his mum coming now, since she'll be here the day of the barn dance. Charlie and Mary at the pub even offered her a room for free, so she can stay the night if she likes. "Hey, they can afford to," Jess had said when she passed on the message to Archie. "Think of all the money they save getting me to skivvy for free when they could be paying someone. . ."

As I shove the corset back in the suitcase, I see Archie has moved on to something else.

"Oh! Please don't," I say, not wanting my friends to see the photo of the soldier.

They all think so little of Auntie Sylvia that it feels like treachery to let them see her precious portrait, her lost love.

"What, what is it?" says Lawrence, clearly sensing it might be something interesting from my reaction.

Jess's already there, staring at it with Archie.

"Who is it?" she asks.

"Please be careful with it," I beg them. "It's Mrs Saunders' sweetheart. He died in the Great War."

"Er, I don't think he did," says Archie, raising his eyes from the photo to look at us all.

"What do you mean?" I ask, frowning at him.

"He didn't die," Archie says plainly. "This – this is your d-d-dad, Lawrence!"

"What?" says Lawrence, grabbing the frame and staring at the young man's face, his dark, bright eyes. "It can't be!"

"Turn it round – see what's on the back," says Jess, scrabbling at the reverse of the frame, flipping the tiny catches so the backboard comes away. "Usually there's the name of the photographer's studio, and sometimes the sitter. Yes! Look – see?"

Three sets of hands turn the frame around. And there, on the back of the photograph, is more than just a name. Written in faded, scratchy copperplate lettering, are *these* words...

To my dearest Sylv,
With love and affection always,
Your Joe

My mind is racing, running, twisting itself in knots to understand this. And Lawrence isn't finding it any easier.

"Joe," he mumbles. "My dad's name is Joe..."

"T-told you!" says Archie.

"And if you still don't believe it, look at this," says Jess, grabbing the picture and now holding up the soldier's face next to Lawrence's. The brown, laughing eyes are the same. There's no doubting the resemblance, scribbled love note or not.

Even Lawrence can't deny it, now that I've grabbed an old rust-spotted mirror and held it in front of him.

"It IS my dad!" he whispers, shocked.

So . . . the soldier in the portrait *didn't* die.

He's Lawrence's father – Joe Wills – and he survived the war and went on to be a farmer.

Mr Wills was Auntie Sylvia's sweetheart.

And now they act like they never knew or liked each other *ever*.

What happened to change—

I pause, spotting that Lawrence, Archie and Jess have gone silent, and are looking at something behind me.

Slowly – with a tight knot of dread in my tummy – I turn and see Auntie Sylvia staring at me, her head and shoulders rising through the attic hatch.

"Would you care to explain what on earth is going on here, Gloria?" Auntie Sylvia asks in a voice so cold and angry it chills me. She's using my full first name too.

"I'm sorry, they came to help me and—"

"I told you before – I don't want you associating with children like this, never mind inviting them into my house and letting them rifle through my private things!"

Auntie Sylvia is right to be angry, I know.

But suddenly I'm angry too.

A coiled-up spring snaps inside me and I can't help the words that come out next.

"You don't even *know* my friends; you won't even give them a chance!" I yell. "Archie has a stammer that everyone teases him about, and so they don't know how kind and sweet he is. Jess is treated like a slave at the pub, and she's lovely to Rich because she has a brother just like him. And Lawrence has to put up with people like you being snobby about his mother leaving, and he can hardly help that, *can* he?"

"Gloria!" barks Auntie Sylvia. "Stop it this instant or—"

"And you're not perfect either. In fact, you're a liar. You said your sweetheart died in the war, but he's not dead and he's Lawrence's dad!"

"Gloria, I did not – at any time – tell you he was dead," Auntie Sylvia hisses at me through tight lips, as if she's struggling to hold her temper.

My own anger fizzles away as I consider what

Auntie Sylvia has just said.

Sure enough, she never mentioned that he's been killed, only that the Great War had got in the way and ruined everything.

I'm no closer to understanding what went on between Auntie Sylvia and Mr Wills, but I do understand that I've made yet another mistake.

A horrible one.

"Children, I'd like you to leave now, please," says Miss Saunders, in as steady a voice as she can manage. "And Gloria, I think it's best if I write to your mother this evening and ask her to come for you and Richard."

My heart practically stops as I hear a plaintive cry from the bottom of the ladder below.

"Glory, Glory, Glory?"

Oh, no.

What have I done. . .?

21

How to Sew a Truce

Me and Auntie Sylvia didn't talk yesterday evening.

We didn't talk this morning.

So I was in no hurry to get back to the cottage after school today.

Instead I followed Lawrence, Jess and Archie as they cut through the churchyard and over the stile.

Together, me and my Outsider friends wandered across the common, half-heartedly throwing overripe damsons at each other and ducking so we didn't get hit.

We climbed the fence and meandered through the strange field of sprouts, which, until I came to Thorntree, I hadn't even known grew this way: like small, branchless trees, dotted with green nodules all over the stems.

Sitting on the fence that overlooked the back field, we watched as Harry drove the tractor and a giggling Lil rode casually on the back bumper.

I'd thought about coming here and talking to her, telling her how it had all gone wrong with Auntie Sylvia, maybe even asking her advice.

But then I saw in the distance Lil lean over and kiss Harry and reckoned my big sister wouldn't be interested in what I had to say anyway.

And so me and Jess waved bye to the boys and walked down the lane that would bring us out on to the green, beside the cottage.

"So, do you definitely think your parents *will* come and collect you before the barn dance?" Jess asks me now, kicking stones along the way.

"I don't know," I reply. "I expect Mrs Saunders will tell me as soon as she hears back from them."

Jess mutters something under her breath. I don't ask her to repeat it because I think it might have been something incredibly rude about Auntie Sylvia.

"Lawrence was really quiet today, wasn't he?" I say instead.

We've all been quite quiet and gloomy after what

happened yesterday. While the whole class gossiped about the film that was shown at the weekend and gossiped even more about the fundraising dance *this* weekend coming, we three were mostly silent, as if we were in mourning.

But Lawrence seemed wrapped up in his own particular black cloud. He hadn't asked his dad anything about Auntie Sylvia yet; didn't want to in front of Harry and Lil and Sally, he said.

"He was quiet because he doesn't want you to go," Jess surprises me by saying. "He likes you too much."

I feel my cheeks burn red. Could it be true? Was Lawrence upset today because of me leaving, as *well* as the secret he'd found out about his father?

Glancing up at Jess, I'm about to ask her more, but then I see she's staring at the ground, a frown that *might* be disappointment on her face.

Maybe she's not such a tomboy after all.

Maybe I was right about her liking Lawrence. . .

"Girls!"

Oh – I hadn't noticed how close we'd come to the cottage. Auntie Sylvia must have seen us and flung the window open to call out to us.

"Can you come in here, please?"

Jess turns to leave.

"No – I meant both of you, please," Auntie Sylvia says unexpectedly.

Shooting me a puzzled look, Jess follows me to the front door, which Auntie Sylvia has thrown open.

My heart thunders, and I can tell Jess is nervous too from the hesitant, birdlike way she's walking.

Are we about to get another lecture? I can't read Auntie Sylvia's face – her mouth is that still, straight line that gives nothing away.

And then I see what she's been doing. Tatters of fabric lie on the floor beside the sewing machine, and hanging from the back of the stair door are two beautiful dresses made of ivory-white parachute silk. . .

Both dresses have sashes at the waist; one is a soft, dusky mauve satin, and one is a leaf-green velvet.

Jess's mouth hangs open.

"Glory, the one with the mauve sash is for you. It will go well with your colouring," Auntie Sylvia says matter-of-factly, though I can't help noticing she's using my nickname again. "And Jess . . . I thought you might like the one with the green sash. I thought it would bring out the colour of your eyes."

Jess stares at the dress, then stares at Auntie Sylvia.

"If you'll accept my gift, of course," Auntie Sylvia adds.

Jess still can't trust herself to believe it. Can't get over someone bothering to notice the colour of her eyes. But I can tell Auntie Sylvia has just sewn us a truce.

"The dress is for you, for the barn dance," I explain to Jess.

She looks at me, tears brimming in her eyes. I don't think Jess has ever had anything new in her entire life, and certainly nothing this beautiful.

"Oh, thank you, thank you, Miss Saunders!" she suddenly babbles, tears spilling down her cheeks.

Auntie Sylvia reaches in her pinny for a clean handkerchief and hurriedly passes it to Jess. Jess pats her eyes, gives her nose a loud honk, and goes over to the dress.

Her dress.

"Can I touch it?" she asks warily.

"Of course!" says Auntie Sylvia. "But be careful of pins. I haven't stitched it all together yet. And there's one more detail to add... Glory, can you go to the attic and fetch my mother's old hat? The one Richard was, er, playing with? I'd like to take the pansies off it and sew them on your dresses as a corsage."

"Yes, of course," I tell her and slip through the door, trying not to disturb our dresses too much.

As I take the steps, I can hear the wonder in Jess's voice as she asks, "How can you make something like this?" and Auntie Sylvia answers, "It's quite simple with a sewing machine. Would you like me to show you how it works?"

I don't know what's made Auntie Sylvia soften, but her mind has changed and I'm so relieved I can hardly stop myself from squealing with happiness. And someone *else* is happy too; as I step up the ladder to the attic, I can hear the clucking of hens and Rich singing, "You Are My Sunshine" to them at the top of his voice.

"Where is it, where is it?" I mutter to myself, searching around amongst the suitcases and packages for the hatbox. At last I spot it, and from the top step I reach out and grab it with one hand, pulling it towards me.

The round box isn't heavy, but it's awkward to keep hold of and tilts out of my hand and down on to the landing floor. Coming to a stop on its side, the hat and tissue paper tip out, while the lid rolls away like a cardboard wheel.

I quickly pad down the ladder to gather it all up, and then hesitate.

More crumpled tissue paper lines the bottom of the hatbox, and now it's loosened and slightly come away. Sticking out from underneath, strangely, is the stamped corner of a letter.

My fingers gently pull the tissue paper back, and I see more of the envelope. I tilt my head and read the address written on it, in scratchy copperplate.

Miss Sylvia Saunders
3 The Green
Thorntree
Essex

It's Joe Wills' handwriting. Same as on the back of the portrait.

What's it doing here? Did Auntie Sylvia keep it in the box for a reason? But why wouldn't it have been in with her *own* things, instead of hidden away under her mother's hat?

And then I look closer still and realize that

something about the letter isn't right.

It's never been opened...

"Jessica had to leave," says Auntie Sylvia, as I step back down into the living room. "She said she'd be needed back at the pub to help with the pig, and washing up glasses for the evening shift. Poor girl."

I'm holding the hatbox, with the letter stuffed in my pocket. I'm about to hand both to Auntie Sylvia, but she speaks first.

"Please take a seat, Glory," she says, ushering me to the settee while she sits herself on the armchair. "Now, I think I might have been a little harsh on your friends. Richard and I have had a good chat today, and he says that they have been very kind to him. Kinder than any other children he's come across, either here or back in London."

"It's true," I agree.

"Very well. I will certainly be more civil to them from now on. Also, I think *we* might both need to apologize to each other for what we said in the heat of the moment yesterday. What do you think, dear?"

"Oh, yes, please, Auntie Sylvia!" I gush happily. "I'm awfully sorry. I know what I did was wrong, but

I don't know why I got so angry. . ."

"Glory, you've been through a shocking experience at home, and then you've had to leave your parents behind in a potentially worrying situation," Auntie Sylvia says calmly, her hands in her lap. "You've managed remarkably well. It's no wonder that you lost your temper. You've probably needed to have a good old shout at something for a very long time."

"I didn't mean it to be *you*, though!" I tell her, feeling a little teary myself now she's being so understanding.

"Well, perhaps we're a little alike, you and I. I think I may have *also* been keeping things bottled up inside."

"Perhaps you needed a shout too?" I try to joke.

"Perhaps I did." Auntie Sylvia smiles back at me. "I'm afraid I just felt very embarrassed when I heard you and your friends talking about Mr Wills. And angry with myself for not keeping quiet about the photograph when you first saw it. I really should have destroyed it years ago."

The impolite question that I really should keep to myself . . . it slips from my lips anyway.

"What. . . what exactly happened between you

and Mr Wills, Auntie Sylvia?"

Auntie Sylvia looks down at her hands for a moment, and I wonder if I've gone too far, asked too delicate a question.

"Joe Wills turned eighteen at the end of 1917, and enlisted for the army straight away," she finally begins, lifting her head and looking intently at me through her wire spectacles. "He asked my father if we could be married before he left, and my father said no. Though Father did say that after the war, if we felt the same, he would reconsider. But Joe obviously changed his mind; out in France, he met a pretty nurse from Manchester. He married her and brought her back to the farm, and I was humiliated. The whole village has been laughing at me ever since."

I want to tell her that's not fair.

I want to tell her I'm sorry it worked out that way.

But most of all I want to tell her she's *wrong*.

"Oh, it's not like that! I really don't think *anyone* is laughing at you. No one remembers or cares or even *knows* about what went on all those years ago. Lawrence certainly didn't."

Auntie Sylvia gives a start, taken aback at the forthright way I'm talking. But I need her to understand something I feel suddenly very sure of.

"Look, I thought Lawrence and Jess and Archie were unfriendly when I first arrived in the village, but I was acting unfriendly to them too," I say quickly, desperate to get my point across. "Don't you see that might be the problem? People in Thorntree just wonder why you're so ... aloof. That's all. I honestly think that's *all*."

Auntie Sylvia blinks at me.

"I ... I hadn't thought of it that way," she stumbles over her words. "That's very ... insightful of you, dear. I shall certainly give it some consideration."

I'm suddenly thrown, all my bravery leaving me now that I've said my piece. I'm just a thirteen-year-old girl sitting across from an older woman, wondering if I've been far too forward in the way I've just spoken to her.

"Sorry," I say in a small voice.

"Not at all, Glory," says Auntie Sylvia, dismissing my worries with a wave of her hand. "And I really am very sorry about what I said to you yesterday, you know. I have enjoyed your company very much, yours and Richard's. You've both been ... a joy."

A joy.

A hard lump forms in my throat at her lovely

words, and now I feel terrible.

I've done something I shouldn't have.

"You might not think so when you see this," I say, remembering the letter in my pocket.

"What is this?" asks Auntie Sylvia, taking it from me as I lean over to her.

"It fell out of the bottom of the hatbox. I think . . . well, I think your mother hid it there. It was unopened – till a minute ago. I read it before I came down. I'm sorry."

But I don't think Auntie Sylvia is listening to me. She's recognized the handwriting, and one hand flies to her mouth as soon as she pulls the letter from the envelope.

"Oh, Joe. . .!" she cries, her eyes scanning the twenty-two-year-old letter, sent from France with love and desperation.

. . . you've never written to me in months, Sylv, and it's breaking my heart. The post is not always reliable, I know, so I'll wait till the end of the year, and if I still hear nothing . . . well, I'll understand your meaning. Perhaps you want to respect your parents' wishes. Perhaps you've found someone else. I don't want this to

be true, of course, but if it is, I'll let you go, if that's what you want...

"I *did* write! I wrote him *endless* letters," Auntie Sylvia practically moans. "Why didn't he get them?"

"Maybe ... maybe..." I flounder, trying to help find an explanation.

"Oh," she says flatly, something occurring to her, I'm sure. "Of *course*. I gave Father the letters to send for me when he went to work, because he said the post in town was more regular and frequent."

"He didn't ever send them," I murmur.

"They disapproved that badly?" Auntie Sylvia says sadly of her parents. "To take Joe's letters ... to take away our chance of happiness. And for what? Ha! Here I am, an old spinster on my own in this cottage, while Joe Wills had an unhappy marriage with a girl who hated the countryside and went so mad with loneliness that she left him and her children in desperation to go back to the city. Oh, my ... what a terrible, terrible waste!"

You know, Rich isn't the only one who's allowed to give out hugs.

I leap up and rush to Auntie Sylvia's side, letting the hatbox tumble from my lap and on to the floor.

"It's fine. Everything's fine," I tell her, as I wrap my arms around Auntie Sylvia and feel her lean gratefully into me as she cries.

"It's going to be all right," says another voice, and Rich appears.

What did he hear? Would he have been able to understand any of it?

But those thoughts are pushed to one side as my brother scrambles on to the arm of the chair with Duckie and Mr Mousey, the three of them joining our cuddle. . .

22

Signs and Stars

"You can open your eyes now..."

I do as Auntie Sylvia says, and stare into the long mirror fixed to the wardrobe in her room.

In front of me is a girl in a simple but beautiful ivory-white silk dress with a mauve sash and pretty corsage of purple fabric pansies.

Her black shoes are glossy with shoe shine, and her long black socks are pulled up to her knees. With the long hem of the dress, they look more grown up, almost like stockings.

Waves of brown frame her face, thanks to the rags that have been tied in her hair all day and teased out with Auntie Sylvia's fingers.

"So, what do you think?" Auntie Sylvia asks me.

"I think *you* look lovely," I tell her, catching sight now of the cornflower-blue dress Auntie Sylvia's wearing. It's a bit old-fashioned, like a long-sleeved flapper style from the 1920s, but it suits her and is miles better than her drab owl uniform of brown tweed skirt and charcoal-grey cardigan.

"We're not talking about *me*, silly sausage," Auntie Sylvia laughs, but I think she's secretly pleased with the compliment. "Are you happy?"

"Yes, yes, I am," I say, turning this way and that, hardly recognizing myself.

What must Jess be feeling right now, as she tries on her own party dress at the pub? I've seen Archie already – he passed the cottage earlier, on his way to meet his mum from the bus. I knocked frantically on the upstairs window till I got his attention, and then gave him a wave and a thumbs up. In return, he grinned and waved the navy striped tie he must have borrowed from Mr Wills or Harry. "Very smart!" I mouthed at him as he grinned and hurried away.

And in a few minutes, just as soon as Rich locks the chickens safely away in their coop, we'll set off for Eastfield Farm, where I'll see Lawrence, and Lawrence will see me.

I get tummy flutters at the very thought.

Does Auntie Sylvia feel the same way about seeing Mr Wills? Or have too many years and too many hurt feelings ruined any chance for them to even just talk and be polite to each other?

"Here..." says Auntie Sylvia, lifting a dainty glass bottle from her bedside table. "It's lily of the valley."

She dabs the cool stopper on my wrists and either side of my neck.

Now I feel grown up and pretty, in a very different way from my sister. And instantly I know that I love Lil, even if we're as alike as sherbet and sprouts, even if she's as flighty as a cabbage white butterfly hovering over the green outside.

"All done! *Readyyyyy!!*" Rich shouts up to us.

"Shall we go to the, ahem, ball?" Auntie Sylvia jokes with me.

"Let's!" I smile at her.

As I turn to leave, I feel an itch on my face and scratch it without looking.

"Oh," I mumble, feeling the pinch on my cheek and the dampness on my finger.

"What's wrong?" asks Auntie Sylvia. "Oh, you've just caught the edge of your scar. Here..."

As she pats my cheek with the corner of her hankie, I look at the smudge of blood on my fingertip, and my heart sinks.

Normally, I don't believe in omens and signs and all that hocus-pocus.

But this ... it's like a flashback to the day of the bomb.

A reminder that happy as I felt just now, terrible things can lurk *right* around the corner...

"Stop. Stop, Lawrence!"

I don't know whether to be cross with him or laugh.

"You know you like it when I spin you fast, Glory," he calls out above the sound of the folk band's flurry of guitar, fiddle and accordion.

"I know I'm going to be sick if you don't let me go," I tell him.

His warm hand in mine, the other pressed into my back ... it's lovely, thrilling. But I really need to get some fresh air.

"Spoilsport," he says with a wide smile, as we wind down to a halt.

Now I can get my breath, I begin to see familiar faces whirl into view.

Reverend Ashton is chatting to Mr Carmichael, my teacher.

Lil and Harry are nearby, huddled close and gazing into each other's eyes, as if it's a slow dance and not a fast jig playing.

Jess – in her pristine white dress – is helping Charlie and Mary from the pub sell beer and lemonade at the table that's been set up by the door.

And there's Rich, clambering up hay bales at one end of the barn with a couple of small boys he seems to have become friendly with this week at school, thanks to Auntie Sylvia's teacherly influence.

As for Auntie Sylvia, when we first arrived, I helped her find both a spare chair and a tucked-away corner where she could sit and happily watch the goings-on without being too much observed herself. In her lap she's holding a glass of lemonade as well as Duckie and Mr Mousey. I bet she's nervous now, waiting for Reverend Ashton to call her up to the piano that's been wheeled out from the farmhouse.

But with a sudden twist in my tummy, I realize there's someone missing. One of the Outsiders.

"Have you seen Archie anywhere?" I ask

Lawrence, as the band end their tune and everyone in the crowded barn applauds madly.

"Nope. He's going to be somewhere here with his mum, though, isn't he?"

I clap along too, but realize Lawrence has left his hand on my back, where it was.

"I'm not sure... He'd have wanted to introduce her to us, wouldn't he?" I suggest. I think of Archie when he passed Auntie Sylvia's, his face lit up full of hope and excitement. I can't wait to hear how he's got on with his mother.

Somehow it doesn't feel right – having fun at this party – without him being here...

"Yeah, maybe," Lawrence replies casually. "Hey, this one's good. C'mon, let's dance again!"

I glance over at the busy, bustling refreshment table and see that Jess is watching us over the shoulders of her customers. She looks ... forlorn, and I can guess why.

"I'm tired. Can't you ask Jess to dance for a change?"

"She's busy," says Lawrence, wrapping both hands around my waist now.

I suddenly feel a little trapped. I *really* need air.

But then I spot Mr Wills talking to Mr Brett, the

grocer. Mr Wills has swapped his farmer's outfit of tweeds and wellies for a dark suit that looks nice, if a little tight. Same as most men here, it's probably his one good suit. Maybe even his wedding suit.

Seeing him reminds me that I should try to speak to Lawrence again about his dad, Auntie Sylvia and the never-received letter. I told him, Archie and Jess about it at school on Wednesday, but Lawrence hasn't said much about it since, just said he needed to think about it before he spoke to his father.

But I don't want to say anything to him here, where we could be overheard.

"Come here," I say, beckoning Lawrence to follow me outside.

He grins cheekily, which makes me uncomfortable. I hope that I didn't give him the wrong impression.

"I just want to talk," I tell him, pushing the door open.

And now I can see someone else has the wrong impression – Jess has just frowned at the two of us, wondering what's going on.

The air has a bite to it tonight, chill wind whipping at my thin dress, and I wish I'd grabbed my coat before we stepped out.

It's pitch-black too, especially once Lawrence

quickly closes the barn door behind us. The only light is a trickle coming from under the rickety-edged wooden door.

"Need a hug to keep warm?" Lawrence jokes some more. At least I hope he's joking. I do like him, but things are suddenly going a bit far, a bit fast for me.

"No, I'm fine," I say, quickly, and take a step back. "I just wanted to talk to you about the letter. Do you think you should speak to your dad about it, since Auntie Sylvia is here?"

I hear Lawrence let out a long sigh, and his silhouette comes more into focus now that my eyes are adjusting to the light.

"Look, I don't think I should. It's ancient history, Glory," he says. "And what good would it do? Yeah, it must have been tough for Miss Saunders, her parents doing that to her. But it's not as if I like her now. Nothing's changed. She's still a snobby old—"

"Oi, Lawrence," says Harry, his head appearing around the barn door, "want to leave your girlfriend alone for a minute and give us a hand to push some of the bales back further? We need to make more room for dancing."

Embarrassment more than cold makes my skin

prickle with goose pimples.

"Coming back in?" Lawrence asks me.

"In a minute," I tell him.

I watch the shaft of light vanish again as the door closes behind him, and now – as if to compensate – the full moon drifts out from behind a cloud.

Outlines of hills and trees and fences and outbuildings become visible.

And – my heart skips a beat – an outline of a figure.

A figure sitting on the gate, hunched over.

My instincts tell me to rush back inside, but then I pause, recognizing the skinny someone and the flop of hair hanging over his forehead.

"Archie?" I call out.

"Hey," he calls back, raising a hand.

"Archie – what are you doing out here?" I ask, hurrying over to him. "Where's your mum?"

Close up, I see he's got his gaunt, stray-dog look about him again. I scramble up on to the gate beside him, realizing only too late that the rust and dirt of the metal will probably stain my dress.

"I waited for three hours, for b-both buses that were due today, just in case she m-missed the first one. But she d-d-didn't come."

"Oh, Archie," I say, feeling his hurt. "Something

must have happened. Maybe—"

"Nothing will have h-h-happened, Glory," he replies flatly. "It'll be the same as last time, and the time be-before. I'll get a letter next week saying s-s-sorry, with a ten-bob note in it. Then she'll tell me about her latest, 'lovely' new b-b-boyfriend, I bet."

I thought all my anger had gone since me and Auntie Sylvia had made up, but another spring suddenly uncoils. How could Archie's mum let him down like that?

"She doesn't deserve to have a son like you," I blurt out, before I remember that sometimes family are the only people allowed to criticize family. But I can't seem to stop myself. "I mean, you're great. Doesn't she know how lucky she is?"

Archie doesn't respond at first; he's just lifts his head and stares at me, his eyes roving over my face as if he's trying to make out my features in the moonlight and memorize them all.

"You look beautiful," he surprises me by saying.

"Me? No, I'm not! Specially not with this scar," I bumble, taken aback. "It's so ugly."

"It's not ugly – it's interesting," Archie says softly. "The f-f-first time I saw it, I thought it looked exactly like a star."

His finger reaches out to gently touch my cheek. I don't pull away.

"A star?" I reply, shell-shocked and thrilled. "Er, I don't think so. And I made it bleed today, so it probably looks even worse."

Archie tilts his head to inspect my altered scar.

"Maybe it looks more like a shooting star now, or a *falling* one from this angle. And they're both m-m-meant to be lucky, aren't they?"

Catching my scar with my nail and making it bleed; I'd thought it must be a sign ... and maybe it was. Could it have been a good sign after all?

A sign that I got it wrong again, in the best kind of way?

I thought I'd fallen for funny, cheeky Lawrence, but now I know as clear as night follows day that steady, sweet, gentle Archie is the boy who's sneaked up on me and my heart.

"Where? Where's the falling star, Archie?" a little voice pipes up in the darkness. "I can't see it!"

"Rich! What are you doing out here?" I ask him, slipping off the gate and down on the uneven surface of the farmyard.

"I came to find you – Auntie Sylvia is doing her songs now. Quick!"

Sure enough, I can hear the strains of "You Are My Sunshine".

I'm not leaving Archie on his own out here, so whether he likes it or not – and I think he likes it – I grab his hand and pull him inside.

The barn seems more crowded and warm when I go back in, and everyone is facing Auntie Sylvia at the piano, swaying and singing happily along to the music she's playing.

At the end of the tune, she smiles shyly as the crowd applauds, and quickly launches into another song, and another.

I stand smiling and watching her, my hand still surprisingly, wonderfully entwined with Archie's on one side while I drape an arm around Rich on the other.

"Glory?" Rich says at one point, and I lean down to hear what he has to say. "I'm a bit cross with Duckie. He made me do something I shouldn't have..."

"What was that, sweetheart?" I ask him.

"He made me tell the farmer about the letter Auntie Sylvia didn't get. That was a wrong thing, wasn't it?"

So my brother *did* hear our conversation the other day, and he understood more of it than I gave him credit for. And now he's blinking up at me, hoping I'm going to say that what he – what *Duckie* – did is fine.

"I don't know," I tell him, being honest. "Maybe—"

"Richard? Richard?"

I'm suddenly aware of Auntie Sylvia calling out, and the people in front of us parting to let him through.

"Ah, there you are – I need my page-turner for this next song!"

The parting of the crowd doesn't just let Auntie Sylvia spot Rich; it lets a visibly startled Jess and Lawrence see that me and Archie are holding hands.

I let go straight away, just as the crowds shuffle back to their original positions, but denser than ever, blocking my view.

"Are you all right?" Archie asks.

"Mmm," I say, not sure if I am. I quickly fake a bright smile and immediately feel the tug and twinge of the new speck of scar that's formed on my cheek.

It's a sign...

Like I say, I don't believe in signs.

But what if it matters? What if...

I give myself a shake back to sense and

concentrate on the pretty tune Auntie Sylvia is now playing.

"*If I was the only girl in the world...*" everyone in the barn begins to sing, their voices swelling and soaring.

At the same time, there's also a shuffling, and a sense that something is happening.

Putting my hand on Archie's shoulder for balance, I peek over everyone's heads and shoulders towards the piano ... and see that Mr Wills is now standing behind a pink-cheeked Auntie Sylvia, acting as her page-turner instead of Rich.

"Didn't expect to see that!" Archie whispers to me. "It's almost as if M-M-Mr Wills knows something's changed..."

"He does," I whisper back. "Rich just told him about the letter!"

And now my brother himself is the sudden cause of chitter-chatter, as Lil shoves him up on to the hay bale stage and swirls him into a waltz.

As the song ends, all eyes are still fixed on Rich and Lil, with everyone oohing and ahhing, commenting on what a sight for sore eyes they are.

Which means only me and Archie spot the surprising thing that's happening over by the piano. . . Mr Wills has just bent down to give Auntie Sylvia a fleeting, tender peck on the cheek.

I'm still reeling at that wonderful scene when I realize people are turning to look and smile at me.

Why?

What's happening?

"Hey, how about 'Land of Hope and Glory' next?" Lil is yelling out to thunderous cheers. "In honour of my kid sister, of course, as well as Her Majesty!"

Everyone is laughing, and when Auntie Sylvia launches into the first chords, the patriotic roaring nearly raises the rafters. It's just as well the Luftwaffe only rely on maps and landmarks and lights. If they worked by sound, we'd have a squadron of Messerschmitts heading our way now. . .

"Glory!" Someone grabs my attention with an urgent tone to their voice.

It's Jess. Her eyes rest on the hand I have placed on Archie's shoulder; then she quickly lifts her gaze to my face. She seems anxious, agitated.

"What's wrong?" I ask.

"It's Rich – he's run outside. He's looking for you, Glory. He thinks you've gone up to the sprout field."

I think how dark it is out there, especially if the moon slips back behind a cloud. And the strange, waist-high spikes of sprouts might look almost comical in the daytime, but they'll be positively eerie now.

"But why would he think that?" I ask her.

"I don't know," Jess replies with an urgent shrug. "I tried to stop him. . ."

"What's wrong?" Archie asks, leaning in to hear, the sing-along is so ear-splittingly loud.

"It's Rich – he's gone up to the sprout field on his own. I *have* to get him."

I'm out of the barn first, leaving whoever's behind me to close the door.

"Glory?" says a figure outside. "I think I just saw Rich in the distance. Here. . ."

Lawrence holds out his hand and pulls me into a run.

What's he doing out here, I wonder, gathering up my rustling skirts in one hand so I can move more easily.

"Don't worry," Lawrence says breathlessly, "we'll find him together, Glory."

"And I'm h–here too," Archie calls out from just behind us.

Lawrence makes a sudden noise that sounds a lot like a cross between a snort and a sigh. But it's probably just because we're running uphill now, up the back field.

"I see him!" Jess's voice drifts in the chill air as she hurries to catch us up. "There – he's climbing over the fence into the sprout field!"

She's right – he looks so tiny and frail, like a stick man, a stick *boy*, now balancing on the fence and holding his arms out wide.

"What's he doing?" I gasp out loud, my chest burning with the effort of running.

"Is he looking at the stars?" Lawrence guesses.

The sky is still dark with clouds, but he's right – pinpoints of bright lights are glimmering.

Only they're not just glimmering; they're *moving*.

"They – they're not stars!" Archie yelps, hurtling past us, as if Rich is the finishing post. "They're NOT STARS!!"

Oh no . . . he's right! What we're seeing is strafing *bullets* glowing orange as they fly through the night sky.

And a rumbling and rattling – which I'd barely noticed in my rush and panic – is getting louder, as the dogfight above us draws nearer. Any second now the fighter planes will blast out from behind their cover of clouds. . .

"Rich! RICH!!" I screech, finally getting my brother's attention as I stumble towards him.

There's another noise now, a cacophony of drones, the moans of air-raid warnings overlapping in the surrounding villages.

"Look, Glory!" Rich calls out to me, holding his hands to the heavens. "The stars are falling! I'm going to catch one, for luck!"

I'm just a few feet from him, but I think our luck has run out.

Thundering behind his head is the looming, growling black monster of a plane, coming down to earth any second.

"This was what the sign meant!" I whisper desperately to myself. "*This* is where we die."

And then the explosion throws me and my parachute dress into the soft, dark earth. . .

Time to Go Home...

Mine wasn't the only parachute in Mr Wills' fields on Saturday night.

There was Jess's, of course, then the ones belonging to the pilot and his gunner, who bailed out and landed in the sprout field.

The two dazed and injured men found themselves surrounded by slightly drunk barn dancers, some brandishing guitars and fiddles – till the partygoers heard their Scottish and Liverpudlian accents and realized the plane that came down was an RAF Bristol Blenheim and on *our* side.

I don't know what happened to the crew members after that, but I do know what happened to me and Rich. Neither of us have much of a memory of being rescued, checked over by the doctor and ferried back to the cottage and put to bed.

What's clearer is that we spent all day at home yesterday, never getting out of our pyjamas once. We were fussed over and mended by Auntie Sylvia, fed sweet treats and hot milk in between, and allowed to read books and comics and play records on the gramophone as much as we wanted.

It would've been like heaven, if we hadn't ached so much.

"Ka-pow, ka-pow, take that!" Rich yelps, dancing around me now as we walk across the green towards school.

"You look like a panda," I laugh.

Which is bad, because it hurts to laugh with my cracked ribs.

"A panda *boxer*," says Rich, throwing fake punches at me.

He arrived at the safety of Thorntree with one black eye, and has now survived two plane crashes (one enemy, one friendly) and has *two* black eyes and a scar over the ridge of his nose to prove it.

"Are you sure you're all right, though?" I ask him, glancing back at Auntie Sylvia, who's chatting to a neighbour about the events of the weekend. "I know she won't mind if you stay off school today, Rich."

"I'm fine, thank you. I like being with Auntie Sylvia," says Rich, starting to skip-hop his way through what's left of the cabbages. Some have been harvested and the more rotten ones simply left to the very last of the butterflies. "Are *you* all right, Glory?"

"Yes. Auntie Sylvia has bound me up nice and tight," I tell him as cheerfully as I can, while delicately patting the bandages under my blouse.

I'm all right about my ribs, and the scratches and scrapes. They're all a bonus, considering I'd expected to die when the force of the crashing plane flung us like rag dolls across the back field.

I'm actually *more* worried about going into school today, and seeing Jess.

I heard she was all right, the least bashed about of us all.

Lawrence got away with just scrapes too.

I'd love to see Archie, of course, but Mr Wills dropped by the cottage yesterday to chat to Auntie Sylvia, and told us that Archie is more or less fine but has possible concussion and might not be at for school for few days.

As for Jess ... I don't know what I'll say to her

when I see her. "So, you lied to me? And you lied to my brother and told him I was waiting for him in the field?"

Rich explained that much yesterday, when Auntie Sylvia asked us to talk her through what had happened the night of the barn dance.

Or maybe I could say, "I didn't know you hated me so much to do that, Jess. Was it just because you saw that Lawrence liked me?"

But that didn't make sense either. She'd spotted me holding hands with Archie later the evening. It must have been obvious right then that Lawrence wasn't the one I was fond of in that way.

Maybe Jess was just angry with me for breaking up the Outsiders by letting feelings get in the way. . .

Whatever her reason, I'll never forgive her for putting Rich in danger. Jess, of *all* people, should know what it's like to have a brother even younger and more trusting than his years.

"Hold on," I tell Rich now, as he nearly walks out into the road.

Typically, he hasn't spotted the bus rounding the corner, drawing to a creaking, grinding stop by the gaggle of villagers waiting to board it and be taken to town.

"Careful, Rich," I remind him. "You've got to keep your eyes open for—"

"GLORY! RICH!!"

The familiar voice . . . it's like the sound of home. You know, it *is* the sound of home.

"Mum?" I call out, aware of the quaver in my voice. "MUM!"

She's just come off the bus, and hurries as fast as her Sunday-best shoes will let her across the rough road, her cobalt winter coat open and flapping like a bluebird's wings as she runs to grab us in her arms.

"Mum!" yelps Rich, jumping up and down as she hugs him.

With streaming eyes, I turn to see where Auntie Sylvia is, and see her blurrily rushing towards us.

"Mrs Gilbert! What a surprise – how lovely to see you," she tells Mum, hovering above us now and looking a little useless. "How . . . I mean, why. . ."

"Our Lil got a message through to us," says Mum, on her knees and clutching us both around our waists, as if she daren't let us go.

"How did she do that?" asks Auntie Sylvia, bemused. "The telegraph poles have been damaged. We had a plane come down and—"

"Indeed, Miss Saunders. But yesterday Lil

persuaded Mr Wills' oldest lad to drive her on the tractor to some neighbouring village around here," says Mum, still locked in a hug with us. "She phoned our local civil defence HQ and of all the luck, her dad was on duty and took the call! And when he came home, of course I'm saying to him, first thing in the morning, Norman, I'm off to Thorntree to see the state of our little darlings."

"Well, that's very enterprising of Lillian – *Lil*," says Auntie Sylvia. "It was quite a nasty experience for the children. What happened was—"

"Yes, the bus driver told me all about it," Mum interrupts, perhaps not realizing how rude that might seem. "And I can see for myself the state my poor babies are in!"

"We're all right, Mum," I try to reassure her, but she's concentrating on Rich, leaning back so she can properly study his battered face.

Rich – who's forgotten what he looks like – just grins back happily at her.

Then I notice Auntie Sylvia is wearing her thin-lipped grey-owl scowl.

"I've tried to take very good care of them, Mrs Gilbert," she says, protectively.

"And I appreciate that, Miss Saunders," says

Mum, her gaze moving from Rich to me as she speaks. "But I'm here now, my poppets. And your old mum will take look after you. Quick as we can, we'll get you both back home, since the country's no safer than the city, it seems!"

Torn: that's how I suddenly feel inside.

It's crazily wonderful to see Mum again, but she doesn't understand how lovely Auntie Sylvia is. And I suppose Mum thinks Auntie Sylvia might not have taken enough care of us, given the way Rich looks right now. But – in spite of our ridiculously bad luck to have been so close to two stricken planes – Mum also has no idea how happy and safe we've felt here these last few—

"Glory – you have to come quick."

It's Archie!

I'm surprised to see him standing over us, looking tired and gaunt, with a cut to his lower lip and a pleading look in his eyes.

"It's Jess; she's on the bus. She's leaving us. She's leaving Thorntree."

His words chill me to the bone, and for a second I freeze, unsure what to think. And then I know what I need to do.

"Mum, I'll be back in a minute," I say, wriggling

free and gasping as my ribs protest at the sudden burst of speed.

"She feels awful, Glory," Archie says as he lopes awkwardly by my side. Obviously something else hurts apart from his head. "She came up to the farm yesterday and had a real row with Lawrence."

"With Lawrence? Why? She adores Lawrence!" I say, without thinking I might be saying something Jess might not want broadcast. Though after what we've been through, maybe there's no time for niceties any more.

"But that's it; she told Rich to go off to the field on Saturday night because Lawrence *asked* her to do it. And she'd do anything for Lawrence."

"It was *Lawrence* who came up with the lie?" I gasp. "Why would he do that? I thought he really liked my brother!"

"He did. He *does*. Lawrence just wanted an excuse to get you on your own. Away from *me*."

I gaze at Archie and realize there was *more* than one argument yesterday. The boys have fallen out too, haven't they?

What a mess!

And all because of *me*...

But I have no time to think about that now, not when I need to get to Jess before it's too late.

"Can I give someone a message?" I check quickly with the bus driver, who's helping someone with awkward luggage.

"Two minutes, dearie," I hear him say as I bound onboard.

Jess's sitting on her own in the third row back. She has her head down; I think she's seen me coming. I slither into the seat beside her.

"Jess, whatever's happened, *please* don't go," I beg her.

"I'm *so* sorry, Glory!" she bursts out, lifting her head up to stare out of the window in the direction of the green and my mum and brother. "Is Rich all right?"

"He's fine – it looks worse than it is," I try to assure her.

I notice she's clutching her gas mask box in her hand, and a lumpy drawstring bag is at her feet. Is that all she came to Thorntree with? Is that all she's leaving with? I don't suppose her new dress is in there. If it was anything like mine, it'll have been too filthy and torn to repair.

"If anything had happened to Titchy-Rich, I'd

never have forgiven myself," she mumbles. "*Or* Lawrence."

I can't believe this is happening. Our little band of Outsiders, it's falling apart, and I don't want it to.

"Look, Archie just told me what happened," I garble fast. "I know it wasn't your fault, Jess. Please don't leave Thorntree because you think I'm angry with you!"

Jess finally turns to look at me, and gives a small shrug.

"It's not just what happened on Saturday night," she explains. "Being round Rich, it just got to me ... it made me sad. I realized how much I miss my brothers and sisters. I want to be with them so badly."

"But why does that mean you have to leave? Can't you just ask Reverend Ashton to arrange a visit? That might make you feel better."

Jess shakes her head.

"It's the pub too. I hate working there, like I'm Charlie and Mary's unpaid servant."

"So what are you going to do?" I ask her.

"Well, I've been saving up my tips from the customers, so I've got my bus fare to town," she tells me, patting her jacket pocket and making it jangle.

"And once I've seen my Tommy and the rest of 'em, I'm going to take the train to London and get home to Mum and Dad and the others."

"Anyone not travelling, kindly leave the bus," the driver interrupts us with a bellow.

And I know then that I've run out of time, that I'm not going to change Jess's mind.

"Meet you back in London sometime?" I say, as I scramble to my feet.

In that moment I spot that she's saved the pansy corsage from the dress and pinned it on her lapel.

"Yeah, sometime," she says with a nod.

"Outsiders for ever?"

I hold my thumb up to Jess – and she presses hers against it, mumbling "For ever."

With that, I turn and hurry off the bus before she can see the tears in my eyes.

"All right?" says Archie, waiting for me on the road.

"Sort of," I say, curling my arm into his and leaning my head on his shoulder.

Then as the bus begins to trundle off, I hear the thwack of a window being shoved open.

"Oi, Hope 'n' Glory!" Jess calls out to us. "Give Popeye a big kiss goodbye from me, yeah?"

I burst out laughing and don't care if it makes my ribs ache all over again. . .

"I really shouldn't have worn these shoes, should I?" says Mum, as we pick our way through the towers of sprouts and away from the wreckage of the Bristol Blenheim, its nose buried deep, deep in the earth.

Rich loved showing the wreckage to her, same as he's desperate to show Mum round the rest of Eastfield Farm. He wants to show her the barn where the dance was and the hay bales he scrambled over with his new friends. He wants to reintroduce her to Harry, and Auntie Sylvia's friend Mr Wills, and see if we can find Lil too, of course.

At least, for my sake, Lawrence won't be at the farm.

He'll be at school right now, probably dreading seeing me, and wondering why I'm so late turning up.

He won't realize I'm leaving for London, same as Jess. He won't have a clue that after this, we'll be going back to the cottage, letting ourselves in the back door with the key Auntie Sylvia told us was under the mat, and packing our things.

He won't know that while he's in afternoon lessons, me and Rich will be standing outside Mr Brett's shop, waiting for the first of the two buses that'll rumble along endless roads and take us back to London...

"You're a real city girl, aren't you?" I joke with Mum, holding my hand out so I can help her climb the fence that Rich has already scrambled over.

"Certainly am," says Mum, hiking her skirt up to make things easier. "Can't think how you lot put up with all this."

She talking about the dried-up cowpats she's avoiding stepping in as we begin to walk through the back field.

"It's not so bad. Look," I tell her, forcing her to stop and take in the view.

The back field rolls downhill towards the farm – where Archie will hopefully be resting on the settee after coming to find me this morning.

And as far as the eye can see, brown, green and golden fields roll on and on, dotted with trees, hedgerows and cows. Everything is so still and quiet and magical ... apart from the small boy running down the hillside with his arms outstretched, yelling, "Wheeee...!"

"He's grown up a lot," Mum says, watching Rich too.

"Mmm," I murmur, thinking that it's true in lots of ways.

My brother just isn't the nervy boy who came here, friendless and scared of his own shadow, so shy he'd rather wet himself than ask to go to the lav, poor lamb. He hasn't even needed Duckie the last couple of days. He set off for school this morning happily leaving Duckie and Mr Mousey at home, flopped together on the dressing table.

My tummy gives a lurch; how will Rich fit in back in our street, back at his old school? Will he end up alone in the playground again, pretending stones are fossils, ignoring the bullies as they tease him?

Though I don't think he's really taken it in, the fact is that Mum means to take us home today.

And I certainly don't think Rich understood that when we waved off Auntie Sylvia as she headed for the primary school, he wouldn't be seeing her again.

Auntie Sylvia had seemed so matter-of-fact, telling us about the key, accepting what was about to happen. But I'd seen her stumble as she'd hurried off. . .

"Is that– is that Lil?" says Mum, suddenly noticing

a tractor chugging into view down below. A figure sitting on the bumper is waving to Rich. And now Rich is shouting something that the whipping wind won't let us hear and pointing up the hill to us.

Lil sees us – sees Mum – and leaps expertly off the slow-moving tractor.

My sister grasps Rich's hand and they both come running uphill towards us.

As we set off to meet them, I laugh at something that's just fluttered in front of us this second.

"What?" asks Mum.

"It was a cabbage white butterfly," I say. "A long way from home!"

Mum suddenly stops, and puts a hand on my arm.

"It's like Rich, isn't it?" she says.

"What?" I mutter, unsure of what she means.

"Rich is a long way from home too. . ." she replies, as my little brother rushes back to her.

"Mum, it's Lil. Lil!" he laughs, pointing behind him as Lil pants and waves her way towards us.

"Rich?" says Mum, dropping down on to her knees and putting her hands on his arms. "You're not coming home to London with me, are you?"

Rich grins at her, his battered face beaming.

"No, of course not," he laughs easily. "I live here!"

Mum wraps him in a quick hug, and then she scrambles back to her feet to envelop Lil in the hug too.

As I watch Mum's face – so sad to lose her little boy for another while, so pleased to see him so happy – I know that cabbage white showed itself to me for a reason.

It was my sign too.

I'm not ready to leave this place either.

Rich still needs me, even if it's less and less as each day passes.

And I want to see what happens with Lil and Harry, with Auntie Sylvia and Mr Wills, with me and Archie.

And Lawrence... I've just spotted him now, hunched on the back of the tractor behind his brother. He's skived school today, then? Maybe he's been desperate to avoid me, after what happened. He won't have expected to see me here now, that's for sure. He's gazing up at us, a hand shielding his eyes from the autumn sun.

I hold up my thumb, hoping he understands my meaning, and that I forgive him.

It takes a second for it to sink in, but then he lifts

his other hand and gives me an Outsider thumbs up in reply.

My smile is so wide it makes the scar on my cheek twinge, *but that's all right*, I think, touching it lightly with my finger.

It's a fallen star, a lucky sign, Archie said.

Who knows what will happen to us, what will happen with our future because of this war – but maybe I can help.

I'll make a wish upon a star that we stay safe, and all live happily ever after. . .

May
V.E. Day

24

Sunshine and Falling Stars

I close the cottage door and breathe in the scent of the early spring roses that fill the tiny front garden.

Out in the back garden, the twisted old cherry tree is giddy with fat pink blossoms. The chickens like to peck hopefully at the dropped blooms, never remembering that they don't taste as good as their feed, or a nice fat worm.

"Here, do you need a hand?"

Lil stands at the gate, offering me an arm.

"I'm fine, thank you, Lil," I tell her, as I notice how much eye make-up she's wearing. She's so pretty, she doesn't need all that gunk around her eyes.

"It's *Lily*, Nana Glory!" she says overly patiently.

"I know that, sweetheart," I tell her, taking her arm after all, since my great-granddaughter *does* like to fuss over me, as if I'm an elderly china doll. "It's a habit that I'm not likely to slip out of at my age!"

I was pleased that her mother, my granddaughter Ruth, named her after my sister.

Not as much as *Lil* was, naturally. She was beside herself when Ruth and her husband Ben Skyped her to show her the baby and tell her the news.

"Are you looking forward to this?" asks Lil – *Lily* – as we make our way around the green towards the church hall.

There're no cabbages or dancing cabbage whites any more, of course. But the flower beds are very pretty, and I saw a lovely red admiral butterfly when I sat on the bench there the other day.

"I'm very much looking forward to it," I tell Lily, looking ahead of us and seeing the sign strung above the road, fixed between the Co-op and the newly renovated Swan. It's a "gastropub" now, apparently, whatever that is.

V.E. DAY: 1945-2015, 70th ANNIVERSARY the sign reads in blocky lettering.

"Do you remember the *actual* V.E. Day celebrations?" asks Lily.

I like that she's curious. She's fourteen and doing a project on World War Two at school just now, so I suppose today will help her with her work.

"As if it was yesterday," I tell her, and smile to myself as I recall the decorated tables in the street, Lawrence helping his dad push Auntie Sylvia's piano out of the cottage, me and Archie dancing and dancing till our feet hurt, not wanting to waste a moment of our time together.

We knew that the end of the war was wonderful for the world, and terrible for the two of us. He'd be staying on at the farm, since his mum had remarried and moved away, and didn't seem much interested in her eighteen-year-old son.

And I'd finally be heading back to London, with Rich...

But we were lucky. Most evacuees went back to their families in London when they turned fourteen, and could go out to work. Auntie Sylvia and Mr Wills wouldn't hear of us leaving Thorntree till the fighting was over. So Archie worked on the farm, becoming a bit of an expert at repairing the machinery when it broke down, while I got a job helping out in the grocer's shop.

"Wasn't it at the V.E. party that Great-Aunt Lil got engaged?" asks this Lil. *Lily*, I mean.

"It certainly was," I laugh, thinking of the scandal it caused. My sister had only known her G.I. boyfriend Vinnie for six weeks – he was stationed at the American base down the road – and next thing he's on his knee proposing to her in front of the whole village and whisking her off to live with him in Wyoming.

I never went to Wyoming, and Lil never came back to visit London – or us here – for years and years. But I've stayed with her in Florida plenty of times since she and Vinnie retired there. She's ninety-two now (can you believe it?) but she's still the same. I bet she'll be celebrating V.E. Day by sunning herself on her lounger by her fancy pool, while Vinnie dozes and snores beside her.

"Was Harry very hurt when Lil left him for Vinnie?" asks Lily, as we walk through the metal gates and into the yard that was once my makeshift school playground.

"Oh, I think he must've been," I reply. "But he was off in the army by that time, remember, serving in the Far East."

We'll miss him today. So many of us from the

old days here together, and Harry so far away in Australia. He's very frail now, but happy enough, Lawrence says, living in his "granddad" flat at the ranch on the vast sheep farm his family still run.

The two brothers talk on the phone once a week, though Harry's so deaf he can hardly hear what Lawrence is saying any more. Though Lawrence isn't much better – ha! He *never* turns on his hearing aids. When he came for tea last week, I had to ask him *five times* if he wanted more cake. By the time he finally understood, his son Jack had come to take him back to Eastfield and he had to eat it in the car.

"Here ... here we are," says Lily, pushing the door open for me.

The racket inside the church hall hits me straight away. The whole village is here, crowded around long tables, some taped music of wartime songs jangling in the background.

I like the red, blue and white paper streamers draped from the rafters, though they're not a patch on the handmade bunting Auntie Sylvia and I sewed together for the celebrations back in 1945.

"At last!" Lawrence bellows from the table where all of my family and friends are sitting. Instead of a wave, he gives me a thumbs-up hello, as usual. "Where have you been, Glory?"

"Making myself beautiful, of course!" I tease him, as Lil helps me into the spare seat that's been kept for me.

"You're always beautiful, my s-stargirl," says Archie, smiling at me.

And I can sense everyone around us smiling at each other too as my darling husband and I press thumbs together. Well, I'm more than happy to amuse them. It's another habit I'm too old to give up! In fact, ten years ago, when Archie and I had the party here for our diamond wedding anniversary, our daughter Sylvie – cheeky thing that she was – went and had a photo of us touching thumbs enlarged and put on the wall of the hall. Can you imagine?

"Isn't this great, Glory?" Rich says, bending over the table towards me. "All of us here together?"

He means the family, of course. He loves to be surrounded by all his nieces and nephews, his great-nieces and -nephews, and *their* children, whenever there's an excuse to get together.

"Yes, yes, it's lovely, Rich," I say, patting his hand. Sylvie laughs at me sometimes, saying I still treat her Uncle Rich as if he's seven years old, not eighty-two.

But apart from the laugh lines and lack of hair, Rich looks much the same to me. He's the fittest of us all as well, going for long walks over the common and the fields every day with his dogs. (I've lost count of how many he's had – and adored – over the years.)

But as I say, we're not ALL here.

I mean, everyone I cared for survived the war, luckily. Maybe it was thanks to my wish, and my lucky star-shaped scar, perhaps? (Though that's quite well hidden these days, due to wrinkles!)

Our parents stayed safe, happy for the rest of their lives in their little corner of North London – though they never quite forgave the three of us for not coming home to them. Though me and Rich did, I suppose ... for a little while, at least.

Little Rich was absolutely miserable being away from Thorntree and the countryside. And much as he loved Mum and Dad – and our cats, Betsy and Buttons – he only lasted a few months before our parents and Auntie Sylvia came to an arrangement and he moved back permanently.

I left with him, since I couldn't stand being away from Archie a moment longer. Reverend Ashton married us on my eighteenth birthday, and we moved into the cottage, since Auntie Sylvia – and Rich – were now living at Eastfield Farm.

Auntie Sylvia . . . my kind, wise owl. . . I miss her so badly today, although she's been gone years now. Not far, though; she and her Joe are buried in a plot together in the churchyard next door, roses twining over them.

And there's one other person I think about and miss, of course.

I never did catch up with Jess back in London . . . nobody had her address. But there were rumours about what became of her. One of my old Thorntree classmates bumped into her in Peterborough sometime in the 1960s, I think it was. Her family's flat was hit during the Blitz, Jess told him, and after the war, like half the East End, they'd been moved out to a new housing estate in the town.

Then around the 1970s, someone in the village heard she'd become a seamstress, and ended up working as a costume maker for theatre shows in London. Fancy that! I often wondered if Auntie Sylvia making her that beautiful parachute dress inspired Jess's choice of career. . .

"Mum!" says Sylvie, from the other end of the table.

She says something else, but it's so noisy in here I

can't make it out. Though I do love that tune they're playing now. "You Are My Sunshine"... Rich will be yodelling along to that any minute, I bet you!

"MUM," Sylvie calls out more insistently. She pointing towards the door.

I shuffle round to see what she's on about.

And then I gasp.

A tall man is pushing a wheelchair into the hall.

The white-haired woman in the wheelchair, she's wearing a leaf-green velvet dress and the most fantastic chunky floral necklace – pansies, they look like – in shades of green and purple.

She's looking around, staring, searching for someone.

Searching for *us*.

"Jess!" I call out sharply, pushing myself out of my seat.

She sees me, my eyes crinkling with pleasure.

I hurry through the hall as fast as my stiff legs will carry me.

We're hugging before I know it, laughing and crying.

"So, fancy meeting you here!" she jokes as we break free to look at each other. "Nothing changes round here, eh? Same music, same people..."

She's looking behind me, and I turn to see Archie, Lawrence and Rich hurrying over, shock and delight written all over their faces.

"And did you keep your promise to me, Hope 'n' Glory?" she asks.

"What was that?" I frown, trying to remember.

"Did you give Popeye the pig a big kiss from me?"

We dissolve into giggles, turning into our thirteen-year-old selves.

I reach out with my thumb and without a second's pause, she presses hers against it.

"*You are my sunshine...*" voices begin to boom around us, as the music is turned up and the villagers sing along.

Sunshine and falling stars, I think, as Rich and we Outsiders gather together once again.

Yes, sunshine, falling stars and these lovely people ... they've always been the bright spots in my life, haven't they?

And what a wondrous, wonderful life...

Acknowledgements

I've always been a history geek – especially interested in the lives of ordinary people – but never attempted to write a historical novel till my lovely editor Helen Thomas said, "Hey, have you ever thought...?" Huge thanks to Helen for nudging me backwards in time!

Thanks also to the Archive Department at Bruce Castle Museum in Tottenham, who hold on file the most wonderful first-hand accounts from local older people who were themselves evacuees. I loved immersing myself in their varied stories.

Two books that also helped me enormously with visualizing and understanding the reality of wartime and evacuation were *Harringey at War* by Deborah Hedgecock and Robert Waite, and the utterly fascinating *Send Them To Safety* by James Roffey of the Evacuees Reunion Association.

Finally, a huge thank you to my neighbours Roger and Bryn, who both took time to talk to me about their own experiences and memories. And an especial thanks to Bryn for reading an early proof copy and putting me right on several important details which would have left me blushing if they'd stayed there!